CONSEQUENCES
A Novel

Tara Dacus

HybridGlobal
PUBLISHING

Published by
Hybrid Global Publishing
301 E 57th Street, 4th fl
New York, NY 10022

Manufactured in the United States of America, or in the United Kingdom when distributed elsewhere.

Dacus, Tara
        Consequences: A Novel
        LCCN: 2019915044
        ISBN: 978-1-948181-84-6
        eBook: 978-1-948181-85-3

Cover design by: Joe Potter
Cover photo by: Jim Inks (New Village Studio)
Interior design by: Claudia Volkman
Copyediting by: Robert Foreman with KA

This is a work of fiction. All names, characters, organizations, and events are fictional. Any resemblance to actual persons, living or dead, or actual events is purely coincidental.

The profits from this book will be donated to the Rotary Foundation and F-S Rotary Foundation.

DEDICATION

To Rotary and all Service organizations around the globe—those whose missions are to leave the world a safer and better for all people.

To Dave, my rock and biggest fan. Your boundless energy to help others inspires me every day. I love you.

ONE

Today felt different. The early morning sun glowed brilliant in a near cloudless sky. A welcome silence and healing warmth enveloped the hospital and community. It seemed like all were holding their collective breath, awaiting something of enormous significance.

Inexplicable. Though it was January second, and the Fairfield community, just outside the San Francisco Bay Area, had suffered through three weeks of wind, rain, and depression, today the weather felt like spring. Even the usually surly security guard at the front entrance to North Bay Hospital wore a glimmer of a smile. There was something in the air.

As the main provider of healthcare for this vibrant, eclectic, and sometimes chaotic community of 100,000, North Bay Hospital and the city it served were rarely tranquil. Most days, hundreds of faces passed from the courtyard through the hospital doors, many numbed by pain or worry, some relieved, most of them just distracted by life. The endless sound of sirens in the background had become white noise.

The fact that three precious babies, all born to different families, would make their entrance today was not in itself unusual. What no one could have known, though, was the dramatic impact these three would make during their lives.

The first of the three families to break the spell and enter North Bay Hospital's unusually quiet entrance that day were Tony and Maria Gonzales. Once inside, Tony gingerly helped Maria into a vacant wheelchair near the front doors and pushed her to the admittance desk. Glancing up as they approached, the seasoned admittance clerk smiled the smile they'd seen so many times since coming to America. It was a smile with the lips but disdain in the eyes. Tony understood. While he resented the judgment passed so automatically, he also understood more than most that respect was earned, and he knew by reading recent articles in the *Daily Republic* that this hospital was struggling financially due to the large number of people receiving free care.

Avoiding eye contact, the clerk accepted Maria's green card and their driver's licenses and began filling out paperwork. She asked them all the requisite questions—address, nearest contact, where they worked—as Maria grimaced in pain. Then came the final question.

"And how will you be paying for the care you receive?" The clerk spoke as if she knew the answer, having heard it from others so many times before.

Tony, forcing eye contact with the woman, opened his jacket and carefully pulled out a slightly soiled and crinkled envelope. When he opened the envelope with pride on his face, her eyes became riveted on its contents. As had happened with others a few times before, Tony watched intently as her expression of shock changed to admiration and then to his favorite reaction, a nearly imperceptible reddening of the cheeks and lowering of the eyes. When she lifted her eyes again, Tony saw newfound respect. She quickly processed the cash, made out the receipt, and with a sincere smile, bid Tony and Maria "good wishes" as a nurse pushed Maria down a fastidiously clean corridor.

The couple had arrived separately three years before from the huge bustling Mexican city of Guadalajara, which had been their home from birth. After schooling, such as it was, Tony had tried to make a living there, but the economy was poor and unpredictable and had become riddled with senseless violence. The cartels were gaining more control over certain sectors, including commerce, so for those who had good jobs, they were most likely related to a cartel. Miguel Gonzales, Tony's resolute but humble papa, was a man who had done hard but honest work as a janitor all of his life and loved his family and God above all else. One morning he told Tony to sit with him after dinner, as he had something important to say to him. All day Tony worried what his father was about to share.

That night, after a special dinner his mama prepared, Tony sat with his father at the same kitchen table where they had eaten well, shared stories, and laughed and cried together since he could remember. His mother, Bella, was standing behind them, her loving hands on her husband's stooped shoulders. Looking at them, Tony realized only now that his father seemed old.

Miguel told Tony he and his mama had three gifts for him. Tony was stunned and only could stammer, trying to convey *they* were his gifts, that he didn't need anything but the love they had always showed him, but his mama said, "Hush, Tony, now is the time to listen to your father."

Miguel began what he had rehearsed many times. "Son, the first two gifts are better than gold. You are twenty, old enough to understand what I say to you tonight. Your mama has written it down for you. If you choose to accept your papa's advice, I promise you, son, it will lead to a contented life."

Tony sat mesmerized, unable to take his eyes off his father's face.

"First, find work you like to do and that you are good at. Work hard, be fair, do what makes you and your family proud, but never be too proud to accept help when needed, and always help others. By this, you will be as good as any man."

Miguel continued, "Second, make many friends, but remember that family and God are always most important. When a man is true to them, and makes what sacrifices are needed to keep them safe and secure, heaven will be his reward."

Tony sat processing what his father was saying, glad that his mama had already written it down for him, as she passed him the artful and precise piece of paper. Bella watched both Tony and Miguel nervously as Miguel stood, walked over to the only sink in the humble, two-room house, and pulled back the clean curtains beneath it. Sitting down on the floor, he reached far behind the sink, feeling for something until he found a small burlap bag.

Miguel's eyes were intense as he sat back down at the table. Tony's mama, visibly shaken, had pulled up the third chair, where she now sat between the two most important people in her life. Glancing at the door as if someone might kick it open at any moment, Miguel began explaining the third gift.

"Tomorrow, my son, you and your mama will leave Guadalajara and go to Mexico City. There, you will meet your uncle, and he will take you to America. I will remain here for now, and when you are settled, I will follow."

Stunned, Tony's first thought was about Maria, the girl he loved and wanted to marry. He couldn't go without her; he *wouldn't* go without her. And why couldn't his father go now too? A million thoughts began swirling in his mind. Where would he go, what would he do, how would he pay for the trip, why was this happening so quickly? Fear and uncertainty began to grip him.

His parents understood the magnitude of the plan that was being laid out for him and ached for how they knew he must be feeling. "Son," his father continued as his mama wrapped an arm around him, "you must trust this plan. There are reasons, and you will understand shortly. We have made provisions for Maria to follow you, if that is what each of you wish, but with a green card, legally."

Miguel lifted the burlap sack on to the table with the care given only to something of great value. Slowly he pulled wide its edges and withdrew three sealed envelopes, one bulkier than the others, then returned the burlap sack to his lap. Each of the envelopes had words written on them. The first had *Maria* written on it. Miguel gave it to Tony and instructed him to meet with her tonight, in secret, and give her the envelope if that was his decision. On the back was a name and address of a person who would help her obtain a green card so she could join Tony in America. Inside the envelope was $5,000. Tony had never seen that amount of money, nor did he ever expect to. In Mexico humble beginnings meant a peasant's life for most. The dazed expression on his face made his father laugh as he said with an uncharacteristic twinkle in his eye, "There is more."

The next envelope had *Mario Gonzales*, the name of Tony's uncle, written on it. Miguel smiled. "This envelope has $15,000 in it. Part of it is for expenses to get you both safely across the border and settled in America. The rest is for my brother to keep."

Their eyes traveled to the next, bulkier envelope, this one with Tony's name on it.

"There is $24,000 in here, to be carefully used and not squandered, to help you start a new life. Mama has her own envelope."

Tony's heart was pounding.

Miguel, now deadly serious, said, "Tony, my cherished son, you must keep what you are about to hear tonight a secret. To tell anyone what you will hear, including your uncle or Maria, could lead to terrible consequences. Do you promise, Tony?"

Tony gave a heartfelt promise, feeling that in the last hour he had transformed from boy to man. "Papa, where did you get this? If I'm to keep such a promise, I must know. And why are you not going to America with us?"

Miguel knew these questions had to be answered. He looked at his beloved wife, who was sitting on the edge of her chair, and then back to Tony. "Two months ago, the Hugo building, where I have cleaned for more than twenty years, rented a space to a new tenant. They didn't have any furniture or equipment for me to dust, but I mopped the floors most nights. They came to the space only occasionally, always bringing bags, leaving with them empty. But every night when I entered to clean, nothing was changed. As I was mopping one night, one area of the wood floor did not have the same smooth finish. I pushed at the board and it popped up, along with the one next to it. Underneath I saw haphazard piles of money, mostly banded together in twenties and hundreds, mostly American dollars. After quickly returning the boards to their original positions, I finished mopping and locked the door on my way out. Over the next several weeks I watched carefully as armed, sharply dressed gangsters with cruel, hollow eyes entered the space and left. I was always careful while changing a light bulb in the hall, vacuuming the carpet, or mopping the wood floor so as not to be noticed.

"Two days ago, on Wednesday, a desk was moved in, and I overheard them say that next Monday, more furniture and equipment would be coming, and they could get to work. So after much agonizing—for you know I've always taught you to be honest—this was probably my only chance to do what a father should do: provide a better life for his son. On Wednesday night, I prepared my mop bucket with a hidden area beneath a false bottom and entered the space. Making sure no one was around, I removed the now very clean boards and quickly filled the bucket area with as much cash as I could. There was so much money under the boards, I knew they wouldn't even notice it was gone."

Looking at his family now, the bravado Miguel originally felt began to melt. Although he was trying to look confident, his brows had narrowed, and the lines on his forehead looked more severe.

"What if you put it back, Papa?" Tony suggested, breaking the silence.

Having considered this himself, Miguel shared for the first time that last night the gangsters had changed the lock. Bella and Tony knew if Miguel disappeared from work the next day, the cartel might follow him for the rest of his life, probably a short life. Maybe the gangsters wouldn't notice the missing cash or might think it was taken by one of their own if Miguel continued his work like normal. Then in a few months, he could join them in America with the help of his brother.

Tony now understood the urgency, as did Bella. Miguel ended by saying, "Tony, you and your mama will leave early in the morning. Be here at 6:00 a.m. Now take these envelopes and give this one to Maria if she chooses to join you." Bella was crying, refusing to go, but Tony knew what the outcome had to be.

Maria lived four blocks away with her parents and six siblings. At eighteen, and a middle child, she had plenty of freedom but often sat on their dusty porch reading books she borrowed from her teacher.

Maria's thirst for knowledge was one of the things that impressed Tony, along with her beautiful eyes and wavy black hair. That's where he found her tonight, on the front porch with a flashlight, reading a book about the history of San Francisco. She smiled, thankful and happy to see him. His expression, though, let her know something important had happened. Taking her hand, Miguel walked with her to a nearby creek where they sometimes went to be alone. They were silent for several minutes until they reached the rock—their rock—where they could sit close and enjoy the comfort and sounds of the creek. Maria was anxious to hear what was on Tony's mind.

"Maria, I haven't said this to you before, but I hope you know I love you." Tony said. He continued softly, "I want you to be my wife."

Tears fell from Maria's pretty face as she reached out to embrace Tony. Her reaction made him more joyful than he'd ever felt in his life.

After a few moments, Tony, holding Maria close, said, "I'm leaving for America tomorrow."

Maria pulled back, stunned. "What will we do? How can we marry? Are you coming back for me?"

Tony, careful not to share too much, pulled out the envelope with her name on it. "Trust me," he said. "You go to the address on the envelope, ask for this man, and he will arrange a green card for you. Now we must decide, without much time to think. You told me many stories of your aunts and uncles who live in California, near Napa Valley. That sounds like a good place to start. What do you think?"

So, several months later, Maria arrived in Fairfield, California, to start her new life with Tony, his mama, and lots of her own relatives, who had taken quite a liking to their new immigrant family. Tony and Maria's wedding was held just outside of Fairfield beside a lovely vineyard in Suisun Valley, near Napa Valley. They met almost two hundred relatives and already felt like they belonged here. The most memorable wedding toast that evening was to Tony's papa, Miguel, who had tragically been killed by gang violence in Guadalajara, shortly after Tony and Bella had arrived in California. Mother and son alone knew the real story.

Over the next year, Maria worked in her aunt and uncle's restaurant. She liked the business side and quickly learned ordering, bookkeeping, and the importance of making customers smile. Tony worked for another of Maria's uncles who ran a large vineyard operation in the fertile Suisun Valley, where vegetables, fruits, nuts, and, of course, grapes were bountiful. Through his hard work and initiative in learning the business, he was quickly promoted to what really interested him—the extensive farming equipment. He liked everything about it, especially how to keep the machinery running. He always remembered his papa's golden advice and had been able to save most of his "third gift."

In the evenings, both Tony and Maria went together to the local adult school where English for Spanish speakers was offered. Maria loved her teacher, who also encouraged her hunger for books, and they became good friends. Her teacher's name was Katie Flannery.

Paperwork done, receipt for payment complete, Tony followed the intake nurse into the maternity ward, where they were installed in a clean, well-decorated room complete with a leather-looking lounge chair. Maria received kind and attentive care from the entire staff, and several hours later, into the world with barely a whimper came a beautiful, healthy baby girls. She had wispy black hair, radiant olive skin, and soulful eyes like her mother. Tony and Maria stared at her, spellbound, each silently promising to love, nurture, and protect her.

As Tony met Maria's gaze, tears flowed down his face. The joy and pride he felt overwhelmed him when he realized for the first time that this little child—his child—would have a good life here in America. His family would live up to his father's sacrifice.

Their personal moment was interrupted by a vicious scream from the adjoining room, incredibly someone demanding a makeup bag, of all things. Recapturing their moment in time, Tony and Maria decided to name their daughter Katie—Katie Gonzales—a name that would earn the front page someday.

<hr/>

While Maria and Tony were in the delivery room, a second couple had arrived at the hospital entrance with a shoeless three-year-old in tow, clutching her rag doll, which had the apt name of Dolly. John, who was about to become a father for the first time, felt more nervous than Trina, his girlfriend. He was dragging her forty-pound bag, trying to watch little Sara, but Trina was obsessed with her missing makeup bag. "How could you have forgotten it?" she kept badgering him. He must have left it in the truck. Their admissions paperwork went quickly, though, thanks to the insurance card she carried. Soon they were on their way to the maternity ward.

The waiting room was down the hall from Trina's room. John and little Sara were directed there by a gentle and understanding nurse. The nicely appointed room included a child-size table and chairs with a toy box next to it. Sara sat and looked straight ahead, clutching Dolly more tightly to her chest, not bothering with any of the toys. She glanced up at John, who looked bewildered himself. Meeting her eyes, his heart melted. Though she was not his biological child, he'd grown fond of her in the year Trina and Sara had lived with him. She was sweet, hardly any trouble—unlike her mother.

John moved from his comfortable chair to the floor next to Sara and patted her on the back. "It's going to be okay. You're going to have a baby brother soon," he told her.

For the first time, she reached for him, dropping Dolly. John held her tight. He tried to remember if he'd ever seen her do this with her mother. He couldn't remember a single time. Sara was a tough little cookie, and he now felt an intractable bond with her.

Trina had already told John she didn't want him in the delivery room with her, in another attempt to hurt him—for what reason, he didn't know. Instead of being hurt, though, he was grateful. The thought of going into the delivery room made him queasy, and he was fine sitting in the stress-reducing waiting room. The walls were light blue with alternating silver-framed pictures of a serene lake and majestic snow-covered mountains. The modern blue-green furniture was a bit weathered, and John wondered how many families had awaited the arrival of their child while sitting here. The wall TV played a barely audible cooking show. Sara seemed content, and John's grandmother, his only close relative, was on the way with a pair of shoes and a jacket for her. When his grandmother arrived, she told John, once again, with her cross expression, that Trina was bad news, as she scooped up little Sara. Wrapped in Grandma's arms, with new shoes and a jacket, the child relaxed. John knew his grandmother despised Trina but wondered if the tradeoff of now having two grandchildren would outweigh her dislike.

Trina was in full-on labor. Her nurse was certainly earning her pay with this patient. She'd stopped demanding John get her makeup bag.

As her nurse silently wished she had called in sick this morning, Trina screamed, "I told you, idiot, that I want more ice chips! Do I have to call your boss just to get a little attention here? Go get my doctor. And get me more drugs! I can't stand this pain."

At one point, half an hour before, the nurse had simply walked out of the room, hoping to find a replacement, but none was available. She steeled herself, knowing the baby would be born soon, and walked back in to more abuse. The doctor arrived, thankfully, and soon a slightly jaundiced baby boy with a great set of lungs and a meth addiction was born.

After his umbilical cord was tied, the baby was placed on Trina's chest. Clearly irritated, she barked at the nurse to take him because she needed rest. At last John was invited into the delivery room. Sara was content to remain with Grandma. He took his baby into his arms for the first time. Trina eyed him, wondering what his reaction would be. She sensed that her future with him would be based on that reaction. And although she didn't want to admit it to herself, she was better off with him . . . for now.

Awkwardly sitting down with his baby swaddled tightly, John said nothing. He studied the fussy child intently. Until this moment, he secretly hadn't been sure the child was even his. Now he knew. The round face resembled his, the ears had his same unique shape, and the reddish hair cemented it. This was his child. Cradling the baby, he felt him twitch, and observed his tiny face scrunch intermittently. John felt a slight tremor through the thin receiving blanket. He looked up to see the nurse watching him sternly. As their eyes met briefly, she looked away and told him the doctor would be right in. Dr. Green appeared shortly, brows furrowed, and motioned for John to follow him to the outer hall. John glanced at Trina, who was now sitting up straight in bed, eyes focused and alert. Carefully laying his baby back in the crib, he turned the corner and saw both Dr. Green and a police officer waiting.

Dr. Green, not used to the luxury of sugarcoating, told John that his son was born addicted to methamphetamine. John was stunned. "What? How?" was all he could sputter as the shock and obvious truth washed over him. Struggling to grasp what this meant, his first thought was for his baby. "Is he going to be all right?"

Dr. Green looked directly at John, flanked by the officer. "We'll be keeping your baby here for several days while we run tests and allow the drug to be expelled from his system." What he wanted to add but didn't was "It's a cruel way to start out in life. How could you allow this?" As they broke eye contact, a siren began wailing in the background. The doctor quickly walked away, responding to another call on his beeper, leaving Officer Osman and John behind. Two chairs were nearby, and John nearly collapsed into one, head in his hands.

"How could I have been so stupid and not seen this? What happens now?" he asked, looking up into the eyes of the officer, who had seen way too much in his twenty-year career.

Pretty sure of the answer, Officer Osman asked John, eye to eye, man to man, "Are you willing to take a drug test?" The answer was mostly what he expected.

"Yes, absolutely. I've never messed with drugs and won't ever. My grandma would kick my ass."

Trina knew she was in trouble when John walked back into the room. Her little habit had been found out. She mustered all her charms she could without her makeup bag. With tears flowing, she promised to do better. "I love you, John. I made a mistake. Please, please forgive me. I can get through this. We can get through this and be a happy family. Look at your son—he looks just like you." Maybe she even believed all of it at that moment. John was putty in her hands; he just couldn't help it.

A nurse entered the room, bringing the form to complete the birth certificate. Neither parent had given much thought to a name, and Trina told John he could name the baby. He smiled at this unexpected gift. Silent for several minutes, he thought about the men in his life whom he'd admired. The name that seemed right was Leonard John Phillips, after his grandpa. It would make his grandma happy. She missed him every day, she always told John. And maybe Grandma's "I told you so" speech about Trina would be cut short when he announced the baby's name. Yes, that would be his name, and they'd call him Leon.

Social Services and the justice system took over from there, ultimately giving Trina the opportunity to avoid jail and get her life back together. Although the drug use would remain on her record, she accepted thirty days in rehab. When she exited the hospital two days after giving birth, heading for what she actually expected would be like a "thirty-day vacation," the maternity ward's entire nursing staff breathed a sigh of relief. Even the devout Catholics among them said silent prayers that Trina would use birth control and not reenter their doors.

Social Services and Leon's pediatrician thought John could bring Leon home in about a week. He was responding well to treatment. Every evening, after work, John would bring Sara and his grandma to the hospital with him. They'd hold Leon, rock him, sing to him. His spasms had subsided, and his coloring after being born with jaundice now had a healthy glow. Sara was enchanted by Leon. She was enjoying spending her days with John's grandma, and as soon as John arrived home each day, she would beg him to hurry and eat so they could go see her baby brother again. John was excited each day to see him too. *Thank heaven for Grandma,* he thought often, as she had jumped in to do whatever was needed.

Wearing a carefully selected blue onesie, eight-day-old Leon left the hospital for the first time in the backseat of Grandma's new Ford Taurus. Grandma and Sara were on either side of his car seat, cooing at him. John, at the wheel, looked in his rearview mirror and couldn't help but smile. This felt like real happiness. He hoped when Trina returned home from rehab, she could be happy, too, and they would have a nice life together. He vowed on the way home that day to ask her to marry him. In the meantime, he had two kids depending on him, and no way was he going to let them down. A soft little tune being hummed in the backseat caught his attention. He'd heard it hundreds of times in his life, and it had always filled him with hope and comfort. His grandmother called it "Grandma to the rescue."

—⁓—

The third baby made his formidable grand entrance at 10:05 p.m. the same day as Katie and Leon. His mom, Maggie Turner, had gone into what she thought was beginning labor an hour before. She called her sister, Dora, and asked her to pick her up at the corner and take her to North Bay. Lily, her longtime best friend and now next-door neighbor at the apartment complex where she'd recently moved, shepherded Maggie's two other young children into her apartment, where they would be safe while Maggie was in the hospital.

Maggie quietly and carefully gathered her pre-packed bag, which included a nightgown and slippers, her favorite photo of her girls (gold-framed), a few incidentals, and a sweet giraffe onesie for Taylor Turner to wear home. The planned meeting place with Dora was down a flight of stairs from her apartment and maybe a hundred yards to the street corner.

She walked—waddled, really—to the bench by the corner, barely making it as another intense pain escalated. Now breathing heavily, gritting her teeth, she wanted Dora to show up now. Where was she? Minutes clicked —it was hard to know how many—with no sign of the dented silver Mazda. Holding her bag close, she opened it to retrieve her flip phone. To her horror, she realized she'd left it back at the apartment on the table, just as another excruciating pain took hold. She could barely keep from screaming and felt herself slipping into panic.

Maggie didn't think she could stand to try and wave down a passing car. But she had no choice. Someone had to stop and help her.

As she stood, she heard *pop, pop* and screeching tires. The sound reminded her of Dora's car. It must be her, but no one was slowing down, and there was a white-hot pressure on her chest as her balance began to falter. Lurching forward, instinctively protecting her ample tummy, she collapsed with a thud. She lay bleeding, semiconscious, on the poorly lit sidewalk by the noisy roadway where drivers were not prone to stop, especially after dark. Through blurred vision, she saw people running toward her. Maybe there was still hope.

Not far from Maggie's apartment was PAL (Police Athletic League), a wholesome and popular safe place for at-risk teenagers to hang out after school until nine o'clock each night. Four young people were walking home together that night from PAL. They heard *pop, pop*—two gunshots—and saw a woman fall to the ground. One of the teenagers, Vince, seemed to know intuitively this wasn't a minor problem. He led the way as they ran toward her. Once there, they knew they needed an ambulance. Vince ran to the nearest apartment, knocked, and yelled for help. No response. He ran to the next, again with no response. Two students waved their arms toward traffic, and a brave soul pulled over. They frantically asked the driver if he had a cell phone and to call 911.

Vince went back to Maggie, took off his Giants sweatshirt, and placed it under her head. Her eyes were open but not focusing. She was trying to say something. With sirens nearing, Vince leaned down and she grasped his hand, squeezing it ever so slightly, whispering to him, "My baby . . ." Then she glanced down. "Thank you . . ."

As his PAL friends watched helplessly, Vince mustered all of his courage and whispered back, "I'll stay close. It's going to be all right." Inside, he prayed that he was right.

The police arrived. Vince recognized the officers who sometimes shot hoops at PAL. In a flurry of adrenaline, he and his friends told one of them what had happened, while the other officer tried to communicate with Maggie. Firefighters and paramedics pulled up together within a minute, along with several more police vehicles.

The firefighters approached Maggie, their experienced eyes assessing the scene as they knelt beside her. They suspected she was in labor, in addition to the trauma she'd sustained—a gunshot to the chest.

The gurney was wheeled over as Maggie locked eyes with the man in the blue uniform, the one with the kind blue eyes. He knew she wanted to tell him something and hoped he was strong enough to keep his composure, knowing these words may be her last. As she was carefully loaded onto the gurney, Firefighter Tom Arthur stayed close. With her hand on his arm, her eyes locked on his, she said, "Tell my babies I'll watch over them always. This one's name is Taylor."

Like a weight had been lifted from her, she closed her eyes and was lifted into the ambulance. Vince, unable to blink as he took all this in, ran to the ambulance with Maggie's bag, which had been left under the bench. Lying on top of the bag was a giraffe baby outfit.

As the ambulance pulled into the emergency entrance at North Bay, Taylor was crowning. A trauma team went into action as soon as the vehicle door opened. Taylor was born right there, technically in the driveway of North Bay Hospital. Relief could be seen on the team's faces as they huddled in the ambulance. The baby had not been injured by the bullet.

Taylor, accompanied by the trauma pediatrician and two experienced pediatric nurses, went to the newborn unit to be checked out. Maggie was rushed to the ER's trauma room.

Forty-five minutes later, after exhaustive measures and with anger in his voice, the head of the trauma team called the time of death to be 10:51 p.m. He threw his gloves in the trash as the rest of the team looked down in despair and resignation, no one willing to meet his gaze. When would this senseless loss of life end? How could people do this to each other? They communicated this without words, just a glance between professionals who had been through this too many times.

Maggie's best friend, Lily, was waiting just outside the ER with her own eight-year-old daughter and Maggie's two daughters, ages six and four. Dora, Maggie's sister, hadn't responded to multiple calls. No surprise. As the glum-faced doctor approached, asking for the family of Maggie Turner, Lily braced herself. Grabbing Maggie's girls and her own daughter, she held them close as they melted together in grief and disbelief.

Dora showed up at the hospital soon after. Lily and the girls were speaking with police and hadn't seen her. She didn't want to face them, so she hid in the restroom, where she broke down. She had promised to take her sister to the hospital—but once again had let her sister down. She'd meant to pick her up and was even on the way when she ran out of gas.

This time, there was no begging for forgiveness, no knee-jerk promise to get clean, followed by short-lived tries. Maggie, the person who always saw the good in everyone, even Dora, was gone. *What will I do now?* she wondered.

Well after midnight, as she peeked out of the restroom, she saw Lily taking the girls out the main entrance, presumably to her apartment. They were huddled together as if the closeness would make things better, make them feel whole again. Dora walked to the nursery to see Taylor. Through the window, she saw a small crib with a blue blanket and knew it had to be him. He was the only African American baby in the room. Only two other babies were in the nursery that night; one probably Hispanic, wrapped in a pink blanket, and the other pale with reddish hair. Both were fussy, but there was not a peep from Taylor. His arms and legs were busy in constant movement, as though he were fighting something. As she looked on, a tall, blond man in a blue uniform entered the nursery, escorted by a nurse who went directly to Taylor's crib. Gazing at the infant, the fireman touched his hand, and Taylor grabbed onto his finger. A faint smile appeared on the man's weary face. Dora wondered if this might be the man who had tried to help her sister. She didn't have the courage to stay and ask.

On the front page of the local *Daily Republic* newspaper was a photograph taken in the hospital nursery of three babies all born on January 2, 1999: Taylor, wearing a giraffe onesie, was flanked by Katie and Leon. The article, which the reporter had struggled to write, told of a mother shot and killed while in labor on a local street corner.

Police were tracking down leads. They had two men in custody, both of them eighteen-year-olds with gang ties.

What the reporter didn't know—couldn't have known—is that these three babies would connect years later. This time they would grace the front page of nearly every newspaper in America.

TWO

John chose his words carefully as he prepared to propose to Trina. They had met the summer before last at Jake's Bar and Pool Hall. She was a waitress there, and about as popular with the guys as the game of pool itself. No getting around it: Trina was a "looker," blonde, great figure, flirty. She loved the adoration. The guys loved her and vied for her attention, but she usually told them she didn't mix business with pleasure. If a guy crossed the line and became aggressive toward her, she knew how to put him in his place with a good-natured barb. That usually did the trick, giving everyone a laugh—even the perpetrator.

Jake's business had increased twofold since he'd hired her, and although he thought she was a pain in the neck sometimes, he put up with her tardiness and her dropping pitchers of beer. The increasing bottom line meant Jake could pay his bills, take some money home, and even take a few days off now and then. He was willing to put up with Trina's idiosyncrasies.

Jake's now had quite a following of regulars, which included the quiet but formidable John Phillips. A strapping young man of 6'2" and 210 lbs., a full head of red hair and immense biceps, no one messed with him. While not model handsome, he had rugged good looks, including a cleft chin and three-day stubble, which were not lost on Trina. For several months John had been coming into Jake's a few nights a week for a couple of beers and an occasional game of pool.

Other than giving her his orders for his standard Bud draft in a cold mug, he hadn't actually spoken with Trina. She had tried to initiate a conversation a few times, but John felt shy around her and couldn't think of what to say, so he responded with a simple nod. It always left her with the electrifying feeling that he wasn't the least interested in her, which couldn't have been further from the truth. Actually, John was enamored with her, admiring the obvious things but also her vivacious personality and quick wit.

Most Saturdays, John was at his family's gun range, just far enough outside of town that the noise didn't upset the neighbors. In fact, many of their neighbors used the gun range, comparing this gun with that gun and judging each other's marksmanship. Oddly, John felt most at peace at the range, once owned by his grandpa. Since his grandpa's passing several years ago, his grandma had run the place. She made enough income to pay the bills and set a little aside each month.

John loved his grandparents. His grandparents had raised him, taught him to shoot, and instilled in him a love and respect for firearms. Grandma was the only one who was a better marksman than John with a pistol and shotgun, and he and Grandpa always felt proud of that. The assault rifle was the gun for bunkers or lunatics, she often chided.

Having a knack for fixing things, John went to work for a contractor, lugging heavy materials on job sites while learning how to pound nails. He made enough to move out on his own to a little farmhouse nearby, which he would call home for many years to come.

Jake's was hopping on Saturday night, near capacity, much to the delight of management. Trina was carrying a tray loaded with seven Coors bottles to a table when John walked in, their eyes meeting just for a moment. As he sat at the bar, a feeling came over him that they had just connected somehow.

He thought it must have been his imagination. Shortly after, Trina brought him his regular, Bud on tap, smiling. *Is she flirting with me?* he wondered, not unhappy with the prospect.

As the night went on, George Strait's latest hits blared, and everyone was having a good time. Jake enjoyed the sound of the cash register. John was trying not to watch Trina, but he couldn't seem to help himself.

Close to closing time, he was about to call it a night and head home. As he stood up, Trina glanced his way. Her glance was followed by a ruckus at the table she was serving, across the bar from John. Two guys in the corner grabbed at Trina, knocking the tray out of her hand. The one with a ragged beard and lumberjack cotton shirt, barely able to stand, staggered forward, intent on Trina, who was apparently the center of their drunken argument.

In three strides, John was in the middle of it. It wasn't much of a fight. Both men were down for the count in a few seconds. Trina went home with John that night, and she and her two-year-old daughter, Sara, moved in with him a week later.

It was John's first real relationship. It was a rollercoaster, up and down, with unexpected turns, and never dull. He loved it when Trina hugged him out of the blue or reached for his hand wherever they went. Although his grandmother said Trina was too possessive, he didn't mind. To him, it felt like love.

Most workdays, John's pickup would pull into his dusty driveway at about 5:00 p.m. Trina didn't go to work until 6:00 p.m., so they didn't need a babysitter for two-year-old Sara. It wasn't a coincidence that Grandma would drop by shortly after six with a homemade dinner, often John's favorite: cheesy meatloaf. The three would sit together and enjoy dinner, making sure Sara ate her vegetables and drank her milk.

Grandma loved spending time with Sara, and though neither she nor John could be considered neat freaks, she couldn't stand a dirty house. Carrying Sara on her hip, softly humming, she'd go quickly from room to room, picking up, cleaning, folding clothing. After a few weeks with little perceptible effort on Trina's part, she pared down her cleaning goal to Sara's room and the kitchen. Items belonging to Trina were sitting on countertops, on the floor, or lying across furniture. She deposited them onto a hallway table. For the first few months, there was an ebb and flow in the size of Trina's stack; then as the months went by her stack overflowed to the floor, engulfing not just the corner but threatening to cut off access down the hall. Even John had become frustrated.

The worst by far, though, was her apparent lack of care for Sara. As John was driving home one rainy afternoon, on the quiet country road one hundred yards from his driveway, he saw Sara on the pink trike he'd bought her. He almost went into a ditch to miss hitting her. As he jumped out of the truck and ran to her, he could see she was drenched and cold, clothed only in her underwear.

He put her into his truck, wrapped her up in his work jacket, and barreled through the front door of his house. Fully expecting Trina to have had an accident, he was shocked to discover her on the couch, asleep. A lit cigarette had fallen out of the overflowing ashtray. Fortunately, the table was metal.

John woke her up and told her where he'd found Sara.

"She's been a little brat today," Trina said. "I told her to watch TV."

John knew better than to tell his grandma about this one. She would never forgive her.

Trina had become increasingly erratic, at times argumentative, and was often late coming home from work. So when she told John she was three months pregnant, the elation of most fathers-to-be was tempered by an unsettling dread.

Somehow, Trina always knew when she was on the borderline with John, and she knew exactly how to make him forgive and forget about her small mistakes. Once again, his rose-colored glasses returned.

—⁓—

When Trina headed to rehab for her court-ordered thirty-day stint to wean her off of meth, they all hoped, including Trina, that this would lead to the happy life they yearned for. Trina blew kisses to John and Sara as they left her at the rehab intake office. Smiling, she followed a staff member through the doors and down the hall to get settled into a room, thinking briefly of Leon. She thought to herself that that hospital had better take good care of him, unlike how she was treated.

Construction work was sometimes slow in the winter, and John, not one who normally liked to be idle, was relieved when his boss called him with the news that he'd have three weeks off. In addition to Sara, he would now be responsible for a newborn. John had his hands full.

Grandma had promised him she would help all she could, and he knew he could count on her. But he wanted to be a dependable parent, a parent his son and stepdaughter could rely on.

After Trina completed her thirty days in rehab, John and Sara sat patiently in the waiting room. They'd left Leon at home with Grandma. As Trina walked through the doors, the same doors she had entered thirty days earlier, she ran to John and Sara. Hugging them both, she then reached out for Sara. Squirming uncomfortably at first, Sara finally softened and put her head on her mother's chest, wrapping her arms around her as if hanging on in a roller coaster.

John swallowed hard, not wanting what he now felt to show. He realized there were two different Trinas, and this was the one he loved. He thought to himself how his grandma had been right about one thing: drugs could be devastating. But John was sure she had misunderstood Trina. Maybe now Grandma would change her mind when she saw the good person Trina really was.

When they arrived home that morning, Leon was the center of attention. John and Sara were delighted when Trina picked him up gingerly and cuddled him. She whispered to baby Leon as they all looked on, "Mommy's home, and I'll take care of you now."

Everyone but Grandma believed that.

John and Trina were married soon after she returned. She quit her job at Jake's, attended Narcotics Anonymous meetings often, and made an effort to be a good mom and wife. The construction business picked up in the area, so John was busy every day. It was hard, physical work, but it was mostly outdoors, which he preferred, and the money was good. He spent any free time he had target and skeet shooting at his grandma's gun range. Even baby Leon was a regular and had his own toy guns and earplugs. The little family was doing fine, and when they needed someone to watch the kids, Grandma was happy to help.

Three years passed. Sara now was in first grade at the country school a few miles away, and Leon was a rough-and-tumble toddler. By all accounts, he and Sara were thriving.

John never missed going with Trina and Leon to the pediatrician, as he always worried that Leon might have lingering effects from the drugs in his system when he was born. Trina would roll her eyes, clearly annoyed, as John explained the same story each time to remind the busy doctor of Leon's birth circumstances. *Can't he just forget about it?* she thought. But she knew she owned it. She wasn't proud of her mistake, but she had worked to make it right.

There was just one problem. Trina was growing restless. She decided to talk with John about going back to work part-time. She knew Jake's was not for her—too many bad influences. But maybe she could find a job waitressing someplace else. If she worked in the evenings, they wouldn't need to pay a babysitter or ask the curmudgeon, Grandma, to help. That might work. And she could save up for a better car.

A week later, Trina was officially on payroll at Denny's. She smiled nonstop, joking with customers and hustling their food to the table as her evening's work flew by. At the end of every shift, her Denny's apron was laden with change and dollar bills. John stayed up each evening, awaiting her return from work. They talked about the kids while she happily counted her tips. Her tip jar was filling fast.

Then, one Friday night, toward the end of her shift, Billy walked in. The shock of seeing him again caused her to lose her breath. She tried to move, to hide somewhere, but it was too late. He'd seen her. Her heart raced and she couldn't speak.

Billy Brennan had been her drug dealer and more, in the "other life."

A $100 bill sat on the table when Billy left Denny's that night. He smiled to himself, considering it more of an investment than a tip.

—✺—

The signs were subtle at first. Trina made excuses for missing her NA meetings. She was late coming home from work. The ample tips she was so proud of dwindled.

Worst of all, Leon and Sara were no longer her world. When the school called Grandma to pick up Sara and Leon, now grades four and one, because they'd been standing by the flagpole for two hours since the bell, Grandma knew there was a problem.

She couldn't reach Trina, and so she called John, who was on his way home from work. John confided that things hadn't been right at home the last few months.

Grandma, Sara, and Leon pulled up in front of John's house as he arrived. They entered together to find Trina sitting at the kitchen table in her wrinkled Denny's work uniform. They watched as she looked up with a vacant expression, as though she were trying to place them, taking a few seconds to do so.

John couldn't pretend anymore. The voluptuous girl he'd fallen in love with was emaciated and hollow. Hoping against hope that she hadn't gone back to using, not wanting to admit it, he'd covered for her the last several weeks. There was no more rationalizing, and now Grandma knew it, too. It was plain to see she'd traded her good life with him and the kids for a heroin needle.

Grandma packed a bag for the kids and took them home with her, while John prepared to deliver an ultimatum to Trina. Either she would agree to go back to rehab, or he'd keep Sara and Leon and she had to move out. Looking noncommittal, Trina hopped into her faded two-door Grand Am, shouting that they'd talk when she returned from work, as dust from the driveway clouded John's view.

When she returned that night, even later than usual, she went directly to Sara's room, closed the door, and slept there. Heartsick and unable to sleep, John understood she had just given him her answer. He thought about how this all would affect Sara and Leon, as he finally fell asleep with a hard day at work ahead of him.

Grandma had made sure the kids brushed their teeth, showered, and were ready for bed by 9:00 p.m. that night. Something was nagging at her, a feeling of foreboding that she couldn't shake. No one broached the subject of Trina, but Grandma knew she was on everyone's mind. She pulled out the trundle bed just for Sara and Leon's visits, complete with Star Wars and Disney princess bedsheets. As she tucked each child into bed, she hugged them tightly. Leon asked if she would scratch his back—his way of keeping her close a bit longer.

Climbing into the middle of her king-size bed that night, the bed she'd shared with her husband for three decades until he died nearly ten years before, she ached for him. He would have known what to do, what to say to the children, how to help John.

She had just fallen asleep when something startled her. Her eyes flashed open. There, standing next to her bed, were Sara and Leon, holding hands, tears silently rolling down their cheeks, eyes imploring her to save them.

She reached out for them. They disappeared. As she sat up, she realized it had been a sad dream.

To be certain of it, Grandma shuffled to their room. They were both sound asleep.

———〰〰〰———

Grandma was up early to fix Sara and Leon a good breakfast before taking them to school. She marveled at her grandchildren's resilience as they cheerfully ate three blueberry pancakes each, and their favorite scrambled eggs she'd made them. She couldn't forget the dream she'd had the night before.

Ready for school, lunch bags filled with enough for two kids each (Grandma didn't want them to be hungry), they piled into her Ford Taurus. Leon giggled in the backseat as he sounded out the words to Dr. Seuss's Cat in the Hat. Sara acted impressed with her little brother's brilliance, winking at Grandma.

As they neared the school, an unexpected sadness rolled over Grandma. The vision of her grandchildren she'd had the night before popped back into her mind. Sara noticed the change of expression on her face and asked if she was all right.

Grandma pulled to the curb by the drop-off and said, "Kids, let's go to the zoo instead of school today. What do you think?"

They grinned, but Sara remembered it was her day to read her report on the California missions to the class. "Can we go tomorrow?" she asked.

Grandma, feeling a little silly, came back to her senses. They all agreed—tomorrow they'd skip school. She made sure they had their backpacks and kissed them goodbye, promising to pick them up on time today when school was out.

But they weren't there.

Trina hadn't gone to work the night before. Instead, she'd met up with her drug dealer and now boyfriend, Billy. They'd made a rough plan to escape the confines of her "boring life," as they liked to call it, and get out of town before the local police closed in.

Should she bring her kids or leave them was the question, one answered by her entrepreneurial boyfriend. "We'll take them with us," he said, to her surprise. Trina was touched that he wanted her kids. It was further proof of his love for her, she thought. But he was thinking about the cover they'd provide, and perhaps the other functions they could perform, outweighing the hassle . . . at least at first.

That morning, she had packed her things, with clothes for the kids and all the tip money she'd been saving for a car. She knew where John hid his savings and, even more important, his .45 pistol, a gift from his grandpa. It all fit easily into the cheap duffel bag she'd just purchased at Walmart.

Trina and Billy arrived at school an hour before the final bell, driving her Pontiac Grand Am. Even though she'd been a frequent visitor to the school, several months prior, the principal didn't recognize her. Trina was incensed that she had to show her ID before Sara and Leon were brought to the office for early discharge. The office personnel were all shocked at the difference in her appearance in a relatively short time and felt uncertain about allowing the children to leave with her. But when the children arrived at the school office, they embraced her. After all, she was their mother.

Climbing into their mom's Grand Am with "Mike's Used Cars" now covering the license plates, they met Billy for the first time. All smiles, he told them they were going on an adventure together. When they asked if their dad and Grandma were coming, the look from their mother told them what they were beginning to fear—something wasn't right. They huddled together in the backseat as the car sped east.

⎯⎯

Long after dark, the kids realized their "adventure" apparently didn't include food. Not daring to ask about the oversight, Sara remembered the extra sandwich their grandma had fixed her for lunch as she quietly opened her backpack.

She cut the ham and cheese sandwich in two and handed Leon half. They ate hungrily and even shared the bag of fig cookies, just now appreciating how tasty they were. Leon leaned on Sara, his head on her shoulder. His earlier sobs, with a heartbreaking plea to go home, had been met with a backhand from Billy, followed by a tongue-lashing from Trina.

When they stopped for gas, Sara and Leon followed their mother to the restroom. It was filthy, with no soap or paper towels, but at least they were away from Billy, so they lingered. Sara begged her mother to take them home, to no avail.

Her response made perfect sense to the muddled mind of a drug addict. "You kids are being so selfish. Billy loves me. Don't you ruin it!"

Leon hung on to every word she said and remembered every part of what happened next. He shouted back at her, "I hate you, Trina; you're not my mommy anymore."

The beating he took was worth it, but when Trina slammed Sara against the wall for trying to protect him, rage enveloped him.

Billy put a painful stop to it.

Years later, during therapy, Leon would share every second of the trauma, and he would smile at the memory of Trina's bruises.

—∿∿—

When Grandma entered the school office, after scouring the schoolyard, she was met by a perplexed principal. She was told Trina had picked them up an hour before. The look of shock on Grandma's face spoke volumes to the principal, who'd felt uneasy about releasing the children earlier. Grandma stepped on the gas of her Taurus in a race back to John's to see if they were there. Her next calls were to John and 911.

John was at work, high on a ladder, when his cell rang. Normally, he'd just turn off the ringer and follow up later, but something caused him to climb down and check.

He called back. Grandma's voice was frantic. Driving too fast, close to home, he was pulled over by a deputy sheriff. Hearing the short version of the missing kids, the sheriff followed John home in hopes they would discover them safe. Instead, they found a ransacked house with all their saved cash and his pistol missing.

Initially, the search process was slowed due to Trina being the mother. If a parent takes their own children, it isn't usually considered kidnapping, legally speaking. But the seasoned deputy was able to convey the scene at the house and what was missing. The school principal also confirmed her sense that something wasn't right when Trina pulled the kids out of school.

At 6:30 p.m., roughly five hours after Sara and Leon had been abducted, an all-points bulletin for the faded blue 1993 Grand Am with license plate AXT234 went out to law enforcement in California.

Unfortunately, the real license plate number had been covered up with the "Mike's Used Cars" sign, and Trina, Billy, Sara, and Leon were already well into Nevada.

John and Grandma, totally helpless, were devastated at the turn of events. All they could do was wait and fret.

—⁓—

Billy and Sara stopped in Winnemucca, Nevada, for the night. The lighted motel sign flashed a picture of a cowboy riding a bull and room rate of twenty-nine dollars. Since the beating he'd received from Trina and then Billy a few hours earlier, Leon's little face had swollen, and he already had a black eye. Sara saw an icemaker on the way to the room and retrieved a bucketful, applying it to his face and the back of her head. Billy pushed the heavy dresser in front of the door, blocking the entrance to the room and, more importantly, the exit. Trina and Billy fell asleep without a word of comfort for the children. Sara and Leon clung to each other, both hurting physically and afraid for what awaited them when the sun came up.

The next morning, they all woke late. Trina saw a McDonald's across the street and brought everyone breakfast. As they sat on the bed with the faded bedspread thrown back on, they ate in silence, Leon leaning on Sara. Trina finally hinted at an apology about the day before, but neither Sara nor Leon was listening.

They were in their own world, back home with Dad and Grandma, safe and sound. Shortly, they were all back on the road, heading further east.

Sara first noticed Billy peeking at her from his rearview mirror early in the day. *Why was he staring at her so often?* she wondered. She and Leon were coloring with the crayons they'd found in his backpack. It calmed them and made them forget their dilemma for a while.

Just before nightfall, Sara read a sign that said "Welcome to Utah." *Are we going to drive forever?* she wondered but was afraid to ask.

They stopped for gas in the small town of Bovine. Billy couldn't help but grin at the town's name, so similar to the name he'd been secretly calling Trina, except that he'd added "stupid." His confidence had risen the farther away from California they'd traveled. He saw a cheap, one-level motel, one of two in the town, and decided they would spend the night there.

He had something else on his mind, too. As the miles had gone by, Trina had regained some of her senses, such as they were. She'd noticed his glances at Sara, glances that lasted just a little too long and that jogged locked-away memories. But the craving that had landed her and her kids in this situation was ever-present and trumped the slight concern she had for Sara's potential well-being.

Billy knew Trina needed a fix. Duct-taped beneath the trunk was part of the stash he'd brought with them. He retrieved it, along with the roll of duct tape, which he tossed on the bed. *A little extra and she'll be out of it for hours,* he figured. The significance of the duct tape was not lost on Trina.

When he handed the stuff to Trina, she grabbed it. He wasn't surprised; he just smirked. She offered up that the kids were hungry and so was she. The Denny's around the corner could make to-go food for them to eat in the room.

He agreed, and as he walked out of the parking lot, on his way to Denny's, she hustled the kids, the drugs, the Walmart bag full of everything she'd packed, including the money and the .45, and they all jumped into the car. But she'd forgotten the key.

Sara and Leon ducked in the backseat as she ran back to the room, praying he'd left it.

He had. It was on the dresser.

As Trina pulled out of the motel parking lot, she saw Billy, who dropped the plastic bag of food and ran after the car. She floored it as the kids cheered. Her adrenaline was pumping. She checked her rearview mirror and saw the backs of Sara and Leon with their arms waving. Both had their middle fingers up as the car sped away.

With a full tank of gas, Trina headed back west toward Nevada, not knowing what to do. If he found her, Billy would kill them, she had no doubt. Going home was not an option. She drove until very late, finally crossing the Utah-Nevada border. At Wendover, she turned south on Highway 93A, feeling safer to be off Highway 80. They found a dingy motel off the main drag, parked on the backside, and settled in.

Trina was nauseous and shaky. Only her fix would make that go away.

The next morning, Leon awoke first. They'd slept in their clothes, with no more spares, and he was hungry. When he pulled open the curtain to see where they were, Sara awoke. They tried to wake up Trina, but she was passed out cold.

Checking the Walmart bag, they found some money and walked over to the motel office. There was a vending machine, which had all sorts of goodies: chips, candy, even licorice. With twenty dollars they paid for enough to fill their hollow tummies. By 2:00 p.m. Trina still hadn't awakened. When they jumped on the bed, she opened hazy, unfocused eyes, yelled at them for waking her, and fell back asleep.

The motel manager pounded on the door at 5:00 p.m., demanding another night's rent. That propelled her vertical. She grabbed the Walmart bag, handed him the last two twenties, and realized they were almost out of money. As she searched the bag for more, to no avail, she remembered Billy riffling through it. He must have taken the rest.

They had enough in small bills to pay for gas the next day, but not enough for another motel room. And Sara and Leon were badgering her for food. Worst of all, she was afraid that Billy was after her.

Trina was overwhelmed. They spent the last of their food money the next morning, while filling the gas tank one last time. The station's Grab and Go had delicious bean burritos, three for five dollars.

In the Grand Am they headed south, hoping to make it to Vegas, where a friend from Fairfield now lived. She was sure she could get a waitress job there. They made it to Tonopah, with another five hours to Vegas. Scanning the area to make sure Billy wasn't waiting for her, Trina parked in front of the only Subway in town, thinking someone might feel sorry for the kids and buy them a sandwich. Sara and Leon climbed from the backseat over the console to get out of the car, stepping gingerly over the loaded .45 perched between the bucket seats.

Standing in front of the Subway, in clothes they'd worn 24/7, and Leon with a swollen face and black eye, the children stopped several customers as they entered, saying they had run out of food and were hungry.

People looked suspicious, and most didn't stop. They glanced at Trina, who was oblivious. The store wouldn't allow them inside, and Leon was desperate to use the restroom. With no alternative, he peed in a bush right in front of Subway.

Someone called the police, no doubt concerned about the welfare of these children. The sound of the siren brought Trina back to earth, and she shouted at the kids to get back in the car.

Rushing, scared, Sara jumped over Trina, already in the driver's seat, on her way to the backseat. Leon followed his sister closely, stepping on Trina's lap with his left foot, the console between the seats with his right. The tragedy that occurred in the few seconds that followed would indelibly alter forever these fragile lives.

In slow motion, replayed in his mind's eye hundreds of painful times over the years to follow, Leon's right foot tapped the barrel of the pistol, spinning it. As he was landing in the backseat, Trina was grabbing for control of the gun. Gun spinning, her finger hit the trigger. The explosive sound a .45 makes in a small space is deafening, but no one in the car remembered it . . . only the crushing result. Trina screamed at Leon, "Look what you've done! Look what you've done!" Clutching her throat was Sara, his precious sister, his protector, the person he cared for more than anyone else in the world.

As law enforcement arrived on the scene, Leon sat frozen in the backseat, Sara's blood everywhere. The horrendous scene was not what they expected from the initial call. Backup and EMT were immediately summoned, but tragically too late for Sara. After determining Leon wasn't physically injured, one of the EMTs, a young woman, sat next to Leon on the curb in front of Subway. He was shaking, pale, and unable to speak. She asked him if he wanted to be with his mom. The look he gave her was one of fear or revulsion, it wasn't clear which. He moved even closer to her on the curb.

Taking statements from Subway customers and employees was Sheriff Morris, thirty-year veteran and well-known leader of the county sheriff's department. With permanently furrowed brows and sun-creased skin, the man had seen much in his career—too much, he often thought. Grandfather of five, his usual detachment was pushed to the edge with this scene. *None of this makes sense*, he thought. Trina was sitting in the back of his patrol car, awaiting her interview. He suspected she was high on something. In all, nine witnesses from Subway described essentially the same account, that of a presumed mother oblivious to her children as they begged for food, then attempting to quickly leave when they heard the siren. As the children jumped into the car, they heard the gunfire.

Sheriff Morris was determined to get to the bottom of this tragedy. As he opened the back door of his patrol car to question Trina, she was crying, the magnitude of what had happened apparently sinking in.

While Trina was questioned at the Tonapah sheriff's office, her

Grand Am was searched. The "Mike's Used Cars" sign covering both license plates was quickly discovered and ownership of the vehicle was ordered. To Trina's surprise, they also discovered a large stash of drugs and money Billy had hidden beneath the spare tire. Within an hour, she'd lost her daughter, her freedom, and this time, her "warm, fuzzy rehab" would be spent sitting alone in a jail cell in the desert, awaiting extradition to California.

Hearing about the small boy's reaction to his mother from the EMT, Sheriff Morris directed her to bring Leon to the office and stayed with him until they could figure out the next move. In a caring and calm voice, she explained to Leon, who still hadn't uttered a word, where they were going. She promised to get him cleaned up and stay with him until things were figured out. He closed his eyes and began to cry softly, then looked up at her and said, "I want my daddy."

THREE

Taylor gripped his social worker's hand. Together, they knocked lightly on the red door of the modern two-story house. There were clay flowerpots on both sides of the porch with an abundance of purple, pink, and white flowers. The doormat said "Welcome," and even before the door opened, Taylor felt hopeful that this place was the one. He readied his most outstanding smile, devoid of two front baby teeth, and stood with perfect posture.

His social worker, Cynthia Garcia, prayed this would be the one for him as well. Of the nearly eighty foster care children she was entrusted to oversee, this little guy, Taylor Turner, was the one she worried about most. More than anything, she wanted to find him a stable and loving home. Over the last six months, there had been back-to-back disastrous placements. Emotional abuse, physical abuse, or just plain neglect were far too common in the life of a foster child, and Cynthia was on a constant mission to avoid or mitigate all she came across.

Cynthia remembered reading the sad circumstances of Taylor's birth, how his mother had been shot while in labor on the way to the hospital. All the information in the file indicated his mom was a devoted parent to his two sisters. When she was murdered, her best friend, Lily, took all three children into her home. She qualified easily as a foster parent.

The additional income Lily earned, through foster stipends, allowed her to move the family of five, including Taylor, his two sisters, and her own biological daughter, from a two-bedroom apartment into an older three-bedroom, one-bath house in the downtown area of Fairfield.

Across her many regular visits to the home, Cynthia had been impressed by the organized and consistently loving way Lily cared for the four children. Holding hands, following Lily, who pushed Taylor in the stroller, they marched to school on time, their backpacks filled with completed homework and homemade lunches. The school validated that the children were thriving, with good grades and Rotary certificates for demonstrating honesty and kindness to others.

As years passed, though, the stress of being a single mom with four children had begun to take its toll on Lily. She was open with Cynthia, and when they had a moment alone in her kitchen, one day, she broke down in tears. She sobbed, telling Cynthia that it was becoming too much for her, and she didn't know how long she could continue caring for Maggie's children. After her tears and a hug from an understanding but concerned Cynthia, she vowed to keep going as long as she could. She cared about the children, really loved them.

All went well for a few months until a frantic call came from Lily. While she'd been frying chicken on the stove, the children had gotten into a fight, a physical one, rolling on the floor. The sound of a heavy thud shocked Lily and she ran to the living room to stop the melee, scolding the children and picking up a lamp that had fallen. She smelled smoke. She had forgotten dinner was cooking. As she rushed back into the kitchen, she found the stovetop on fire. It spread to the side cabinets, and to the ceiling. She screamed for the children to get out of the house, as she sprayed water from her sink nozzle.

It was too late. The fire was out of control.

The fire department arrived a few minutes later, sirens wailing, the engines taking up half the block. They made sure all the family members were safe and proceeded to pour water on the fire until at last the flames were extinguished, leaving the smoldering, smoky remnants of the house they'd called home. Several firemen came to check on the children. They tried to be reassuring and calming. One tall fireman with blue eyes and graying, blond hair, patted Taylor on the back and told him he was a very brave young man.

Looking down, seemingly lost in thought, Taylor sat up straight. As his suddenly confident eyes looked up to meet those of the kindly fireman, the five-year-old said, "Yes, sir . . . I got this."

Unable to hide his smile, the man patted him on the back again and responded, "I believe you do, young man. Yes, indeed, you are someone special."

A few minutes later, the fireman returned to ask the special and brave young man if he'd like to help them hold the fire hose as it sprayed the last remnants of smoke.

As the scene was being mopped up, Lily and the children sat on the front steps of the neighbor's house, watching. Responding to Lily's call, a professional-looking young man, wearing a crisp red shirt with a roundish gold and blue pin on the lapel, approached the family with furry teddy bears in hand. Lily recognized him. It was Brock, her insurance agent, with an office just a few blocks away. With the bears distributed to each appreciative child, Brock sat next to Lily with his laptop. She was dazed, still trying to get a hold of what had happened. She'd lost her car in the garage, and literally everything in the house was gone. Except for the clothes they had on and her cell phone, they had nothing.

It had only taken him a few minutes to get there by foot, the quickest way, since the street was blocked by first responders. Brock had checked her coverage before he hustled out of the office and was relieved to see she had opted for renters' insurance. It would allow her to financially recover, though he knew from experience that the emotional trauma would take more than money. As he conveyed the comforting financial news to her, she leaned on him and sobbed.

At least this part would go right for her, he thought. After they talked, as he got up to leave, Lily called Cynthia.

She was at the end. She couldn't do it anymore. Cynthia would have to pick up Maggie's children.

Taylor's sisters had been through trauma before, losing their mother when they were six and four. They both remembered parts of it. Many times Taylor would hear his sisters, smiling, talking to each other about their first mom, how she'd taught them to count, how she'd laughed with them at the park. He was mesmerized most of all when they talked about how she wrapped her arms around them, all warm and snuggly. He often wondered what made that hug so special, and he wished he could have had just one. One day he heard them talking about the sad look on the doctor's face when he told them their mom had been shot and he and the medical team had tried really hard to save her . . . but she was gone. *"Gone?"* they'd asked the doctor. "When will she come back?" The doctor had looked to Lily to explain the unimaginably hard news to them. Taylor watched his sisters as tears rolled down their faces. *Gone* was a scary word to them, and now to him, too. He was glad Lily was their mom now. She had been their mom for five years. She was the only flesh-and-blood mom Taylor had ever known.

Cynthia pulled up to the scene in her ten-year-old dark blue sedan. This was the part of her job she hated, the part that made her count the years until she could retire. As she sat in her car, mentally preparing, she envisioned how this would play out, like so many situations before. Normally, there would be days or weeks to prepare for a move, including mountains of paperwork, but sometimes immediacy was required. She knew this process of taking children away from their family created a dire, everlasting memory for them, even in cases where abuse was evident. She wondered what it must feel like not to be wanted.

So once again, Cynthia steeled herself, opened the car door, and walked to the neighbor's porch, where they were all sitting, still watching the last few firemen mop up the scene. Lily started to cry as she told Maggie's children that they would be okay, that she loved them but just couldn't take care of them anymore. She would come visit them; she wouldn't be "gone" from their lives. The girls cried, too, and hugged her, hoping this wasn't really happening.

Taylor sat motionless, taking it all in, wondering if the tall fireman was wrong, that maybe he wasn't special or brave. Maybe that was why she didn't want him anymore. But the fireman had looked him in the eyes and patted him on the back when he talked to him. Taylor trusted him to know.

The adjacent county had a Children's Receiving Center for children who were beginning their journey into the foster system or transitioning within the system, as Taylor and his sisters were doing. The well-planned center, with limited finances and way too many recipients over the years, had grown used and tired. The once-colorful beanbag chairs were little more than shapeless, uninviting lumps of plastic. The worn, stained carpet seemed to tell a story of profound anguish and life's dumbfounding disparity. It had affected countless children who had walked through these doors. Taylor and his sisters gripped hands and looked down, staring at nothing as they entered the center with their fierce advocate, Cynthia.

The hope was that she could eventually find a loving home with someone who would take all three children, but reality told her that would be a tough find, even in Solano County, where foster homes were more prevalent than in many surrounding areas. Short-term homes were commonly used and preferred over institutional housing for children in crisis, but none were immediately available. It was mostly kind and well-intentioned people, schooled in helping traumatized children, who opened their homes for a few days or weeks while more permanent homes could be located. As the children were getting settled in the center, Cynthia's cell rang, giving her good news for the girls, that an interim home had been located.

They didn't have space for Taylor, though. He would spend his first night at the center, without his sisters, comforted by only his soft cuddly teddy bear and the memory of the tall fireman.

It isn't easy to be brave, he thought, as he nodded off to sleep.

Biological family is usually the first place social workers reach out when foster transitions are necessitated. Taylor's father, Michael Bruno, had been in prison for nearly six year on a three-strikes weapons conviction. A reluctant gang member since high school, trouble seemed to follow him. The need to be wanted and a part of a "family" that watched each other's backs won out over his internal compass. Like his own father, at barely eighteen he was sentenced to his first stint in Solano County Jail for drug possession. Released after one year for good behavior, he told himself he wasn't going to follow in his father's footsteps anymore; he was determined to change his course. With the help of a parole officer, he found nightshift work, driving a forklift for a candy manufacturer.

He liked the work and somehow made it there on time, though the bus route often took over an hour. If the weather was decent, he walked, taking about the same amount of time but saving him bus fare. Making a little over minimum wage, with no car to get to and from work, and sleeping on a cousin's couch, his good intentions soon turned south. He was back in jail six months later, this time for two years.

Michael spent his two years well. The jail had classes inmates could sign up for to help them develop skills that had the potential to turn their lives around when they were released back into their world. That's where he met Maggie Turner. She helped facilitate two of his programs, "Thinking to Change" and "Transforming Tools." Even without Maggie's presence, he would have been in those rooms, but when Maggie was there, he sat front and center.

"You know right from wrong. You just have to make the right choices," she would say to him whenever he seemed to lose his confidence. "You can do it, Michael. I have faith in you, and the Lord does too."

Maggie was a "no nonsense" person. She had a job to do—a calling, really—and that was to make a difference in her students' lives that would last after they were released. She took it seriously, knowing she had an uphill climb, with 70 percent recidivism nationally. Unbridled patience and understanding were her weapons of choice, but she was quick to take a student to his knees when necessary. With Michael, unlike some in her charge, she felt certain of the determination and mindset to change direction.

The respect she'd earned from her students made this step rare.

Over the two years, an unexpected bond formed between Michael and Maggie, one borne of respect, friendship, and hope.

When Michael was released, he couldn't stop thinking about Maggie. She'd forced him to be real, to cut through the crap, and to realize for the first time in his life that he had goodness as a human being, that he had an innate ability to help others. She believed in him, and he began to live up to her expectations.

The "success plan," made prior to his release with his jail counselor, included residing at a halfway house in Vacaville, away from his old gang ties. A menial, walking-distance job was secured for him, and the peace Michael looked forward to most was a volunteer opportunity at the local homeless shelter. He was determined. Maggie's faith in him, her belief that he could succeed this time, spilled into every aspect of his daily decision-making, fueling him for the next day. And the most uplifting aspect of this transformation was he had begun to believe it too.

The first time he saw her outside the program, one Sunday at Vacaville's First Baptist Church, was startling to both Michael and Maggie. Maggie was walking by him in the sanctuary, carrying one daughter still in diapers, wearing a pink, frilly dress and holding the hand of another in purple frills, both of them neat and well-behaved, no husband or partner to be seen. As she glanced to her right, there, seated in the last row, nearest the exit, sat Michael. Their eyes met, and both made sure to run into each other at the end of the service.

Neither had reached out during these many months since Michael's release, though both of them had felt a spark. Maggie knew the inherent inappropriateness of this feeling, and Michael was fearful of rebuke from the one person he held on a pedestal. Still, a spark is a spark, and sometimes it simply can't be extinguished. Later that afternoon, as Michael walked three miles across town with a dozen yellow roses in hand, and knocked on Maggie's door, he could hardly breathe. Her smile, upon opening the door, meant everything to him, filling his hollow heart with hope.

Michael understood that this relationship was tenuous, based upon his commitment to stay on the good path. He didn't worry, though. This path felt right to him. Having Maggie and her girls, people to love and protect, was worth whatever he had to do. He met with the parole officer on time, every time. He adhered to the curfew at his halfway house, never missed work, and avoided the places where he was likely to meet up with past bad influences.

One year after release, Michael was the poster child of success stories. His employer, who had signed on to hire him more as community good deed, had happily given him two significant raises due to his hard work and dependability. His release requirements fulfilled, Maggie's tough standards met, he proudly bought himself his first car, packed his few belongings, and drove to Maggie's apartment. She and the girls stood in the front doorway, smiling as he walked from his car up the apartment complex steps. Michael's heart beat fast as he took the steps two at a time, dropped his bag, and reached for Maggie. He embraced her, and she returned it. Love felt real to him for the first time.

Michael took them on a surprise trip the next Saturday, to a place where he'd only been once as a child and had always remembered fondly, the Oakland Zoo. He wanted to see his three girls smile.

They took the little train that stopped at all the major animal enclosures, laughing at the antics of the orangutans, in awe of the tigers and lions, and spellbound by the herd of elephants. He ended the day with a special dinner at a popular fish restaurant on their way home, and he soon learned that he was not the only one who was giving surprises that day. Right before dessert, Maggie, with a joyful smile, shared that she was expecting his baby.

That night, as Maggie slept, Michael by her side, he couldn't take his eyes off her. He was afraid that if he fell asleep, when he awakened this all would turn out to have been a dream. Pastor John's message last Sunday was on being grateful and Michael, to his core, was now a believer.

Life settled in for the little family. Maggie, showing her baby bump of four months, was busy with her job at the jail. Michael was offered overtime at work, and he gladly accepted the opportunity to earn extra money so he could purchase a wedding ring for Maggie.

One night, as he left work, he noticed two guys sitting in a gray sedan parked near his car. When he looked over at them, they nonchalantly looked away, seeming to avoid eye contact intentionally. He thought something felt off. As he pulled out of the parking lot, he watched their lights go on, and in his rearview mirror he realized they were following him. As his mind raced, he decided to drive to the place he least wanted to be—the police department. There, he parked in a visitor space and watched as the car slowed down, started to turn into the lot, then backed up and drove away.

After several minutes, Michael drove home in a roundabout way, making sure no one was following. He thought about getting a gun. It would be a major parole violation for him to possess a firearm. The consequences, he knew, could be devastating. As he walked to their apartment, having parked two blocks away for safety, he considered whether he should tell Maggie. He found her sitting next to the tub, giggling with the girls as they took their bath. He couldn't tell her.

The next day, he left early for work. His boss approved his request to leave work an hour early. At 4:00 p.m. sharp, he exited through the back door at work, sat on a bench under a massive oak tree, and watched the traffic around the parking lot. About forty-five minutes later, in a different model car, the same two guys were perusing the lot. They stopped at his car, then slowly moved past it and parked near the exit to the lot. One of the men, Hispanic, maybe twenty-five years old, looked vaguely familiar

Then it hit him: the man was in a rival gang from his past life.

As he sat hidden under the tree, he tried to think through what he'd learned in his programs in jail. What would they tell him to do? What would Maggie tell him to do? Why were these guys even here? Michael was full of questions with very few answers.

With no way to slip past their car, he decided to confront them, man to man. He reasoned that if he spoke with them, told them he'd been out of the gang for three years now, with no intention of going back to that life, they'd leave him alone. Several employees had gotten off shift and were walking to their cars, so Michael decided, *Safety in numbers. It's now or never.* He walked through the lot, directly to their car, making sure not to surprise them.

Just as he was a few feet away, with his hands up in a peace offering, the driver's door swung open and the familiar young man hopped out, gun pointed at Michael's face. The sidekick approached him from behind, jamming a gun into his back, pushing him forward.

The fight that ensued was quick and lethal. The driver was on the ground from Michael's crushing kick to his right side. His gun had fallen from his hand and as it hit the pavement, it discharged.

Employees in the parking lot were running for cover, calling 911. Michael was on the ground, grappling with the driver for control of the gun, as he heard first sirens in the background. Through brute strength, Michael finally wrestled the gun away from the driver and pointed it directly at the man. He glanced sideways for the other guy and saw, to his horror, that he was lying in a pool of blood a few feet away.

This was the scene as the police arrived, with Michael holding an unregistered Glock on a man while another lay dead from a gunshot wound.

The justice system was swift for a three-strikes case like Michael's. His court-appointed attorney was unable to convince the jury that he hadn't shot the man. The verdict was first-degree murder, with a sentence of life without parole at a federal prison. His son-to-be, Taylor, was due to be born in two months.

After the fire and removal from his foster mom, the biological option for placing Taylor with his father was impossible, Cynthia knew. She reached out to Dora, Maggie's sister. She was in a rehab program for substance abuse but indicated an interest for later, after inquiring about the amount she'd be paid by the foster program.

Striking out with Taylor's biological family, Cynthia began reaching out to adults who knew Taylor. She visited his school, spoke with his teacher, the principal, the school secretary, to determine if any of them could open their home to him and/or his sisters. While all were sympathetic and apologetic, none were able to say yes. The pastor at the church where Lily had taken the children on Easter and Christmas each year agreed to put a general description of Taylor in their newsletter and on the church bulletin board, in the hope that someone could take in the child. Pastor Johnson told Cynthia not to get her hopes up, though. Already exhausting her go-to list of reliable and seasoned homes, her possibilities dwindled.

Taylor woke up each morning at the Children's Receiving Center with his teddy bear firmly in grasp. A revolving door of sad little souls passed through this center, some shell-shocked by single events, most molded by years of chaos and abuse.

Cynthia came to see Taylor the third day, not to give him the good news she'd hoped for, but to provide some comfort and hope. She was surprised to see him playing Legos with another boy about his age, smiling and talking. Careful not to interfere with a bonding opportunity for them, she sat close, curious about the topic that had created such a positive interaction.

Taylor was absorbed as he told the story of the fireman who had patted him on the back, telling him with conviction that he was special and brave. He recounted how the man had let him hold the fire hose as they put out the fire together. Cynthia covered her mouth to hide the smile on her face as he elaborated about helping the fireman save his sisters. Taylor's new friend, Samuel, was mesmerized.

That night, Taylor and Samuel were assigned beds next to each other in the big sleeping room. The two gave each other high-fives, both clutching their teddy bears. After shower time and teeth brushing, cozy in donated flannel pajamas, the children prepared for their 9:00 p.m. lights-out.

This was Samuel's first night sleeping in the center. Taylor assured him it would be all right, though he dreaded the initial deafening silence each night, which was always followed by the sounds of sniffles and soft crying. With no distraction, each child faced their own predicament by themselves.

Hearing sobs from Samuel, Taylor quietly crawled out of his bed to stand next to him while the sadness washed over him. He patted him on the back, remembering how that had made him feel when he'd met the fireman. Reliving those moments, he told Samuel, "You are brave, and you are special, just like me."

The next day, Cynthia came to pick Taylor up. She helped him gather his possessions in a plastic sack from Raley's Supermarket with room to spare. As they walked toward the exit, he turned around and ran back to say goodbye to Samuel.

A solitary tear rolled down his friend's cheek as Taylor whispered something to him. A smile replaced his sad face as he nodded. Cynthia shook her head in astonishment at this young child's compassion.

A male bed had opened up at a home in Fairfield, and she had reserved it for Taylor. The home had recently opened their doors to foster children, approved for five, in addition to their own two teenage boys. As Cynthia and Taylor pulled up to the house and parked, his face deflated. He looked at the front yard, which had a four-foot chain-link fence and barely any greenery, just a white decorative rock in a dirt space dotted with prickly weeds. Taylor looked over at Cynthia, who evaded his penetrating gaze, pretending to be writing something in the folder with his name on the front.

He wasn't letting her off the hook. She finally faced the music of the disappointed six-year-old. "Can I go back to the center?" he implored.

She didn't try to explain things, to share with him about the requirements the foster program maintained, for timing of placements. She didn't tell him that the center was underfunded and couldn't house children for more than a few days. Most of all, she couldn't tell him the system was so overloaded with need that the standards required to be a foster home kept sinking. While most homes were good, a few were exemplary, and many were borderline; this one was, at least from the front, clearly the latter.

She simply told him, "Let's give it a try."

His new caregiver answered the doorbell on the third ring. Mrs. Barry smiled at Cynthia and then, as an afterthought, glanced down at Taylor, who observed her intently. She had dark circles around her eyes, light brown hair, a pocked complexion, and a large lizard tattoo on her upper arm. As he looked past her into the living room, there were four young boys sitting in a row on the floor, three gripping their knees to their chests. Two bigger, white boys were lying on the couch, absorbed in a football game.

Cynthia's gut told her not to leave him, but she had no choice. She couldn't return him to the center and she had no other place she could take him. She'd keep looking, but for today, this was it. She and Taylor followed Mrs. Barry down the hall of the four-bedroom home to the room he was told he'd be sharing with two other boys. There were two trundle beds, each with a flimsy mattress underneath. A set of dingy sheets, along with a pillow past its shelf life, sat on the floor next to a bed. Taylor was hoping they weren't his.

—⁓—

Two months later, Taylor was anxious for Cynthia's next monthly visit. He'd barely said a word at her last visit, due to Mrs. Barry hovering by them.

The day before, Mrs. Barry had squeezed his face, holding it close to hers, reminding him of the consequences for telling. Her over-the-shoulder glances, while Cynthia was there, kept Taylor quiet. Like the other boys, he received free school breakfast and lunch, but on weekends they mostly went hungry. Sometimes a bag of pretzels or chips would be left out for them.

Taylor hadn't told Cynthia about this. He hadn't told about the multiple punches in the stomach, or how he'd been lured to the roof with two other boys, only to have the ladder he'd climbed to reach it removed for hours, to teach them a lesson.

This time, he determined, Cynthia was going to hear all about it.

He was brave, and she heard him. All five of the boys were removed from Mrs. Barry's house that day, and Taylor hoped she would go to jail. He never wanted to see her again.

―――

Cynthia had been contacted by Taylor's aunt, Dora, who now had been clean and sober for two months, after her third trip to rehab. She had stayed in contact with him and his sisters while they lived with Lily. His sisters had been in the same home for a few months now and seemed to be doing all right. Moving them didn't make sense to Cynthia, but maybe with one child—Taylor—and weekly oversight, Dora would be able to care for him.

Dora agreed to all the requirements, including weekly drug testing, the parenting class at the adult school, and a monthly stipend. Cynthia made a careful, written, day-by-day plan with her. It started in the morning with when they'd get up, how to use an alarm clock, when to leave for school, when to get Taylor from school, when and where to buy food, what she would prepare for dinner, and how to do it. On her own time, over and above what the county paid her for, Cynthia worked patiently with Dora. She had brought an alarm clock and a "healthy and simple" illustrated recipe book from her own home.

It was after 8:00 p.m. that night when Cynthia left their apartment. As she was walking to the car, she was exhausted but feeling good about how the day had gone. Taylor stood on the second-story balcony of the affordable housing apartment complex, watching as she opened her car door. She looked up at him and waved, but he didn't wave back; he only stood there, watching her leave. She really prayed that this would work out for Taylor.

The alarm clock buzzed at seven the next morning in the sparsely furnished one-bedroom apartment. Dora and Taylor each slept in their own twin bed. Taylor appreciated having a bed with a mattress, as he'd spent the last few months sleeping on the floor at Mrs. Barry's.

In a Target bag next to his bed, he found a pair of new jeans and a long-sleeved striped shirt that still had the tags, compliments of Auntie Dora. With good intentions, she had made the trip after he'd gone to sleep. She had picked up the grocery items on the list and then decided to go to Target and get something new for Taylor to wear to school. Sitting together at the kitchen table, they both smiled as they ate the sausage-and-egg biscuit sandwiches she'd microwaved for them. Taylor stopped eating only when every crumb was consumed.

In the voice of a six-year-old, but with wisdom far beyond his years, he reassured her, "I will help you, Auntie. We are going to be okay. I'll be good, so you don't have to send me away."

He hugged her and found a napkin she could use to wipe away her tears. They were the tears of a thousand tries. Maybe she could do it, stay clean and take care of Taylor.

Taylor needed to be at school fifteen minutes early each morning in order to get his free breakfast—his second of the day—and he and Dora were ready on time. They walked down to the parking lot as she searched her giant purse for her car keys. At last she found them, and a few minutes later she dropped him off in front of the school, Taylor proudly wearing his new striped shirt and jeans.

As school ended that day, Dora was sitting on a bench by the first-grade classroom. She had taken the time to look through the cookbook Cynthia had given her, and she had carefully turned down some of the page corners for easy reference to those pictures that looked good to her. The title of the book, *Easy Delicious Recipes*, sounded fine, but she wasn't sure how "easy" they were after reading the recipes.

The parenting class Cynthia had enrolled her in started next week at the adult school only a few minutes away. She was familiar with the school. It was the one where she'd tried to get her GED what seemed like a million years before.

The bell rang to signal that school was out, and within seconds the tranquil setting ignited with a flurry of children, parents, teachers, and whistles. Dora watched the door of room number five, where children exited as the teacher, Mrs. Chan, gave a coveted star stamp to each child's hand on their way out. She'd begun to worry that maybe this wasn't his classroom after all, until the last child in line came into viewIt was Taylor. His eyes were searching through the chaos for a warm, familiar face, afraid to show disappointment if none was there. When he saw Dora, his face lit up.

She hadn't let him down. Day one: check.

With thirty-three students, Mrs. Chan had little time to focus on one child, but she took the scene in today and counted this as a good sign for Taylor. The principal had filled her in about Taylor's recent challenges, and they were making a concerted effort to be observant, just in case. Somehow, through it all, he had retained a sweet nature. She was pulling for him.

Over the next few weeks, life began to take on a feeling of normalcy for Taylor and Dora. They had a routine. They would wake up at seven, take a shower, get dressed, and walk to school. Dora's car was giving her trouble, and most days she would walk to his school to pick him up. They'd walk home together, talking about their day.

On the way home, one day, for the first time, Taylor reached for Dora's hand. She held his hand in an awkward way, wanting it to feel comfortable but not sure how.

He had something important to ask her. "Can you tell me about my mommy?"

Dora froze, speechless. She instantly released Taylor's hand and crossed her arms over her chest, staring straight ahead. As they walked without talking, Taylor was confused. Had he done something bad, by asking this of his auntie? Why did she seem mad at him?

As they neared their apartment, Dora regained her composure and asked if he'd like to play at the park, never addressing his simple question. They stayed at the park until almost dark, Dora sitting on a bench looking detached and sad, while Taylor played with other children, glancing her way often to make sure she hadn't abandoned him. That night, with Taylor fast asleep, she dressed and quietly sneaked out, looking for the only thing she'd ever found that made her guilt and anxiety disappear.

Taylor awoke the next morning to an empty apartment. He got himself ready for school, hoping Dora would walk in the door. She didn't, so he left by himself, remembering to grab his backpack. He knew the way.

The last bell rang as he turned the final corner, crossing the busy street by himself. He knew Auntie had more important things to do than walk him to school. Head down, he entered his first-grade classroom just in time to shout, "Here," as his name was called. He hoped lunchtime would come soon. He was hungry.

When school was over, he stood outside his classroom, waiting for Dora. She'd been there each day to greet him, even when he was the first child out the door, but not today. While waiting, he observed all different types of people picking up his classmates. Some were young, some old, some black, Asian, white, Hispanic. Most had smiles for their child, a hug, kind things to say, a pat on the back. What he wished for most, right then, was someone to hold his hand. He sensed it wouldn't be Dora.

As the last few students disappeared to waiting cars and parents, Taylor realized Auntie Dora wasn't coming. His tenured teacher had been keeping an eye on him as she prepped for the next day. He was one of her all-time favorite students, always kind to others, anxious to help, and an infrequent visitor to the proverbial "thinking chair," reserved for those first-graders who had made a poor behavioral decision. Things had been going well for him, it seemed, since he'd been with his aunt, but today something didn't feel right. The fact that he was late this morning, unaccompanied by an adult, and now, at the end of the day, had no adult to take him home, didn't bode well. She walked out of her classroom and over to Taylor, who sat under a tree.

Mrs. Chan reached out her hand to him. He looked up, startled. Had he said out loud what he wished for? It didn't matter; he grabbed her hand. They walked hand in hand to the office. He skipped; she smiled.

Cynthia showed up at school as the principal was finishing her busy Friday, hoping to leave soon. Taylor sat on the floor by her desk, busy coloring a book full of zoo animals he'd never actually seen. As Taylor was leaving the office with Cynthia, the principal followed them out, handing her a sealed envelope. Figuring it was standard paperwork, she tossed it on the passenger seat with a pile of folders. Taylor buckled his seatbelt, and they drove the short mile to Dora's.

As the apartment door opened, Dora looked up at them with a shocked expression. Her speech was slurred, her pupils dilated. On the kitchen counter was the opened cookbook Cynthia had given her, along with chopped broccoli, carrots, and what Cynthia knew with a glance were drug paraphernalia.

Dora told the social worker she was trying. But her car broke down. She didn't have pans to cook the dinner.

Cynthia and Taylor went to the bedroom and used the Target sack to gather Taylor's belongings once again. He made sure his teddy bear was in the sack.

They had been sitting in the car together way too often. Taylor knew Cynthia was making calls that would determine what would happen next, to, or for him. He wasn't sure what it would be.

While on hold with her supervisor, she reached over to the envelope given to her earlier by the school principal. As she silently read the contents, she glanced at Taylor in the backseat. The letter explained that a local firefighter had made an annual presentation to first grades. Afterward, having lunch with her at the school cafeteria, he shared with her that he and his wife wanted to be foster parents. Deep in thought, Cynthia folded the note carefully and put it back in the envelope as she finished her conversation with the supervisor.

A male bed was confirmed with an emergency placement home she knew to be exceptionally kind and experienced. She wouldn't have to drive him to the center, as she'd feared she would. This would be better for him.

—⁓—

A week later, on a beautiful Saturday morning, Cynthia and Taylor were standing on the front porch with the red door. The smell of freshly mown grass mixed with lavender in the flowerpots.

Over the fence, Taylor saw the top of what looked like a swing set. His smile was bright. He knew who would be opening the door . . . it was Mr. Arthur, the tall, slightly graying fireman who had told him he was special and brave. His wife had a warm smile and a plate of warm chocolate chip cookies.

Mrs. Arthur offered her hand to Taylor, and he readily accepted it as he entered the well-kept home for the very first of what would be thousands of times. He understood that they didn't have children; he would be their first. Yes, Taylor knew they had a lot to learn, and he would be patient.

He felt sure this was where he was meant to be.

FOUR

Katie avoided holding her mother's hand as they walked the several blocks to their favorite destination, the Fairfield Public Library, where they'd enjoyed countless visits. She was almost eight years old and had decided she was too old to hold her mother's hand, though she still longed for the comfort of that feeling of security. Maria, her slightly chagrined mom, glanced over at her child with a fusion of pride and sadness. She was growing up so quickly, maybe too quickly.

As they entered the library, Katie placed the five books she was returning on the shelf and smiled at Mrs. Stone, the normally stern-faced librarian. Mrs. Stone smiled warmly at Katie and winked. "Some new books arrived yesterday that I bet you'll find interesting. Want to take a look?" She said this without sounding patronizing.

Maria was grateful to Mrs. Stone for the special treatment she always gave Katie. Over the last few years and many library visits by Katie and her mom, Mrs. Stone had observed how the child reacted to her library.

Katie was polite, for one thing. She was quiet and thoughtful as she meticulously considered the books to check out. And once she selected her books, she held them as though they were unearthed treasure.

Mrs. Stone held Katie Gonzalez and her mom in high regard; she only wished more children who entered this sanctuary appreciated it the way they did.

Katie eagerly followed Mrs. Stone into the preteen section. The only hard decision for her was which books to select for this week's visit. Mysteries and animal books were usually her favorites, but Mrs. Stone was hoping to broaden her horizons. The new books were biographies of significant leaders, movers and shakers, humanitarians of the country and the world.

As Katie carefully perused her many options under the watchful eyes of Maria and Mrs. Stone, she decided on two. They would be her first rudimentary glance into a world that would fascinate her for the rest of her life: American and World History. She chose biographies of George Washington and Joan of Arc.

Maria, an avid reader herself, chose a book on business accounting. She was still working for her uncle and aunt, the same job she'd had since coming to the U.S. almost ten years before. They owned a small but popular restaurant in downtown Fairfield named ZXZX. Every day, except Sunday, the couple arrived at the restaurant before sunrise, cleaned, mopped, washed last night's dishes and pans, and prepped for the day at hand. Maria loved them like parents and worried that they worked too hard. She did her best to convince them to hire others for the menial jobs, but they were adamant. No one was up to the standards they set. So Maria arrived at six each morning to help all she could, then briskly walked the two blocks to their rented three-bedroom home at seven to awaken Katie and get her to school by 8:15. She returned to the restaurant to help until 2:30 p.m., when she picked up Katie from school. Most days, Katie went to the restaurant with her mom after school, where she would sit doing homework and reading until her dad, Tony, arrived to take her home after his long workday in the fields of nearby Suisun Valley.

Each day, when Tony arrived at ZXZX, his favorite part of the day, Katie would run to him with a delightful squeal. Maria would stop working long enough to watch as Katie embraced her dad, both of them lost in a moment of bliss. She was daddy's girl, no doubt about it. That day, she gathered up her schoolwork, along with her library book on George Washington, in her Minnie Mouse backpack. Tony noticed her bookmark was already midway in the book.

As he put the key into the ignition of his 1992 Toyota pickup, both occupants safely seat belted, Katie asked him the first of many questions, as was their ritual. "Daddy, why was George Washington a hero?" Her questions over the last year had become more difficult to answer and had spurred his own thirst for knowledge. He had to stay one step ahead of his daughter, and he feared the day when his only answer would be "I don't know."

This question, though, he thought he could handle. "Maybe it was because he was brave and a man who was trusted," he said. "People were willing to sacrifice everything to follow him in hopes of a better life, because he was willing to sacrifice with them."

Stunned at his own words, he thought of his papa, who had sacrificed his life so he could have a better life in America. His father was his hero.

A momentary sadness swept over Tony as he remembered his father and the simple life he'd shared with his family in Guadalajara. Drugs and gangs had ripped his family apart, and he loathed both. He was determined to keep his family safe.

Katie snapped him back to reality with her next question as they pulled into their driveway. "Daddy, what makes people trust *you*?" She had a troubled look on her face.

Tony turned off the engine and sat still for a moment, the eyes of his prodigious and slightly vexing daughter on him. "Yes, good question, Katie. What makes people trust one person and not another?" He sensed this was one of those important moments. This was a question he had to answer carefully, taking it seriously, not telling her what she wanted to hear. But before he could answer, Bella, his mama, who shared the home with them, yelled her greeting from the side yard.

Tony was relieved as Katie opened the door and ran to her grandmother, who was holding something up. He'd have more time to consider his answer to her question. He was happy for that.

Katie hugged her grandmother, who was careful not to cause her to lose the grip on her cane. Her faded apron had bulky pockets, just right for harvesting her bounty. Bella was happiest in her garden, and today the banana peppers were perfectly ripe. She would make Katie's favorite dinner, Bella's stuffed peppers filled with meat, cheese, and fresh jalapenos. Tony liked the biting hot habaneros, so she would prepare those separately.

Her garden included all sorts of peppers, including poblano, cayenne, the pungent red torpedo, hot lemon, and of course the favorites she'd grown in her homeland: jalapenos and habaneros. Tony brought home every imaginable fruit and vegetable from his work, freshly grown, but still she liked to grow her own peppers. Each plant received her loving, adept care, the knowledge from which flowed through her veins from countless generations before. She hoped Katie would love growing peppers, too, hoped she would feel that same need to pay homage to her past.

In the ten years she'd been in America, Bella had not learned English. Maria had insisted that they all speak English to fit in better from the beginning, and she had enrolled all three of them in an English for Spanish Speakers course, their first of many. Bella tried, but even with continued prodding from her daughter-in-law, she couldn't make the transition as Maria and Tony had done. So they reluctantly spoke both languages in the household.

Most evenings, Bella, a superb cook, made dinner for Tony and Katie while Maria worked at the restaurant. They'd sit around the table, laugh, and tell one another about their day, often reminiscing about stories of Mexico and loved ones. Tonight, while they enjoyed enchiladas with fresh peppers, Tony was ready with his answer to Katie's question from earlier in the afternoon.

"Katie," he said, "you asked me today about trust. It is a very important question, and I wanted to think about it before I gave you an answer."

Bella listened intently. Although she still couldn't speak much English, she'd learned to understand it quite well.

Tony continued, "I think trust is something that can only be earned by doing what you say you'll do, by following through. It doesn't matter how much money someone has or how little. We can all earn trust and lose it. Earning it is much harder."

Bella, normally quiet in these conversations between father and daughter, added in Spanish, "Trust is truly earned when there is a cost to doing what you say. I don't mean only dollars, but what's much more important . . . your time, your hard work, or even, my little angel, your life." Bella looked intently at Tony. "Your dad and I," she said in a soft, melancholy voice, "trusted your grandfather to send us to America for a better life."

Katie's brows were furrowed, and Tony knew another question was coming. Before she could ask, Tony added, "One thing to remember, Katie: when something very important is happening, make sure you have someone you can trust by your side."

"Daddy, I need to ask one more question. The book said George Washington crossed the freezing river for the first time. Then why did the soldiers go with him?"

Tony hoped he wasn't over his head already with his near-eight-year-old. He thought for a moment. "A great leader does thousands of little things to earn trust. Then, when a big thing happens, people trust the leader will make the right decision. Now it's time that I trust you to clean the table and help your grandmother with the dishes."

Katie smiled and cleared the table, content with her dad's answers. That night, she dreamed she was standing at the front of a small wooden boat with soldiers rowing across a perilous river.

Bella finished putting the handwashed dishes away. Her hip ached, as it did most of the time, but tonight it felt almost unbearable. Never complaining, she hobbled down the hall to her bedroom, where she collapsed into her cushioned recliner. She considered again going to a doctor for help with her painful hip, but being undocumented she was fearful of the consequences. She comforted herself by running her fingers lightly over the thinning gold locket she wore, as she had done countless times. It was the locket her husband had given her as a wedding present almost forty years before. It made her feel as though they were still one and, for a brief few seconds, not alone.

⁓

When Bella and Tony crossed the border, hidden in a box truck carrying vegetables, they were fleeing for their lives. The time it would have taken to go through the process of immigrating legally, as Maria was able to do, would have cost them everything. The recent immigration law changes were confusing, but Tony had heard he might be eligible to obtain "legal status," something he and his family prayed for daily.

Though he paid taxes, worked very hard, didn't get into trouble, and took care of his family, he knew he was at risk of being deported at any time. His family had heard of similar situations in Fairfield, where the door had been kicked in at midnight and undocumented people had been dragged out of the house with their children watching. Being "legal" meant he could buy property, obtain a driver's license, earn higher wages, and get in a long line to become a citizen. Perhaps, most importantly, he and his family could sleep better at night.

The process to become legal included costly attorney fees, but Tony and Maria had lived frugally. Most months they were able to save a little money, and Tony still had hidden $11,000 of the money his father had given him. So, one Thursday morning in September 2008, Tony, Maria, and Bella sat in the office of immigration attorney Betty Lam. On the wall behind her orderly desk was a handsome crystal plaque. It was engraved with the word *Rotary* at the top, and the words *In grateful recognition for your dedication to the community*, followed by her name. Several framed diplomas and accolades surrounded the impressive plaque.

Betty began by giving an overview of the new law, as it might apply to them, emphasizing whom it might include. Tony, she felt confident, would be eligible to apply to be a permanent resident, by virtue of two criteria. First, thanks to Tony's papa, Maria had gone through the legal immigration process and was a permanent resident, and the fact that she and Tony were married meant he was eligible, providing the second criterion was met.

The second criterion was essential. To be considered for permanent residency, the individual must not have had any run-ins with the law.

Tony proudly expounded, "I've never had any trouble with the police—no tickets, not even parking tickets."

Bella, however, didn't fit the first criterion now in place in the new law. She was an in-law of a permanent resident, therefore not eligible. Betty gave them hope, though. Once Tony became permanent and perhaps even a citizen of the U.S., that tie to his mother would enable Bella to qualify, providing the law did not change again.

Betty explained further that the cost for Tony's application would be three thousand dollars—fifteen hundred up front and the rest when their application was approved. It was not her first rodeo; Betty watched for the nonverbal response and was relieved to see they didn't flinch at the cost. She had bills to pay, too, and working pro bono for every worthy case didn't keep the lights on.

Betty went on, now energized that she had a paying client, explaining that the application was by no means a guarantee, as the immigration system had an annual cap of roughly 400,000 applicants nationwide. Seeing the look of disappointment on their faces, she added with a surprisingly confident grin that her success rate was excellent. She knew what Immigration wanted, how to present the proof they demanded, and how to complete the daunting application in full.

It wasn't rocket science, she thought, but she was always amazed by how few of her colleagues understood those simple requirements. To cement the deal, she added that until their application was approved, they didn't owe the last half of her fee.

The contract for services was signed on the spot, to start the life-changing process toward a more secure future. Bella hugged her son tightly, glanced up to thank God for answering her prayers, and touched her locket gently. The disappointment on her own behalf was overshadowed by what this would mean to her son.

—∿∿—

Maria's back and arms ached as she unlocked her front door at home. It was well after 10:00 p.m. She'd missed getting to read to Katie yet another night—time together they both cherished. The dishwasher/busboy she'd encouraged her aunt to hire, earlier in the week, had dropped a timeworn plate during the dinner rush of a paltry five customers. Her aunt fired him in a tirade, with customers watching. Once again, Maria was left to scour the twelve metal pots, fifty-plus plates and utensils, clean the stoves and bathroom, and mop. Her aunt and uncle worked hard, too, but over the years were depending on her more and more. That night, it hit her as never before—this was not the future she wanted.

Maria picked up the mail at the post office each day for her aunt and uncle. She'd noticed several letters, some quite bulky, from the Internal Revenue Service in the last few months, but hadn't felt comfortable asking about them, nor had it come up in conversation. As she delivered another one to her aunt, her reaction to it shocked Maria. Her aunt threw it on the floor and stomped on it, then, without opening it, tossed it in the garbage with yesterday's dried food.

So, the following week, when Maria's aunt called her, crying hysterically that she thought the IRS had taken all the money from their bank account, causing checks to bounce, she felt dismayed but not shocked. The landlord had already delivered a notice to vacate as Maria dropped Katie off at school. She kissed her goodbye and told her to study hard.

As Katie exited Maria's 1995 Toyota sedan, she looked back at her mom. Her expression was a rare one for Katie, but it said so much: "Please don't go; don't leave me here today, Mommy."

Maria was conflicted in that moment, needing to get to the restaurant. She wanted to stop the car and take Katie to work with her, but she knew today was not the day for that, so instead she tried to give her a reassuring look. As she drove out of the parking lot, she looked back. Katie was still standing in the same place, looking forlornly toward her mom's car.

Maria had learned to follow her gut instinct in life, as she did in following Tony to America, and with Katie. So she turned the car around, parked, and went back for her daughter.

Something wasn't right. She found Katie sitting by herself in front of her classroom, clutching her backpack. She bolted to her mom as soon as she laid eyes on her. Her reticence at holding her mom's hand only a few weeks back was gone. The two clasped hands as Maria knelt by her daughter, now really concerned about what was going on. "Katie, tell me what's wrong. What's happening to make you feel this way?"

Katie carefully removed her library book from her backpack, *Joan of Arc: A Short Biography for Kids* by Kate Sweetser. It was torn and dirty. Pages had been ripped out. Maria knew it wasn't Katie's doing.

Katie started to cry as she told her mother what had happened, how two girls had pushed her down and taken her lunch and her book right out of her hands, laughing as they stepped on the book and threw it at a tree. With no adults in sight, she had run to the tree to gather what was left of her book, only to be kicked in the back. "You better not tell," they had threatened her.

Gingerly lifting the back of Katie's shirt, Maria saw the dark bruise—not that any further proof of what had happened was necessary.

Maria was so angry at what had happened to her child she could barely speak. The anger was peppered with guilt at how little quality time she'd been spending with Katie recently. This had happened to her yesterday! And it took Maria until today, this moment, to find out. Maria closed her eyes, trying not to cry. She held Katie close and thought how she'd allowed her job, such as it was, to take precedence in her life. She called Tony, but his phone went to voicemail.

Maria and Katie walked to the principal's office. She told the school secretary, trying to stay calm, "My daughter was kicked in the back and had her lunch stolen yesterday, along with having her library book destroyed." Maria pulled up the child's shirt to show the ugly bruise.

The principal wasn't in until tomorrow, she was told, but the secretary could start the incident report. She looked at the child with sympathy as she asked the requisite questions. Katie didn't know the girls' names but gave a good description, explaining it had happened well before school started the prior day, before most students had arrived. By the secretary's expression, Maria guessed she knew who the girls were.

She pushed redial on her phone. Tony's phone went to voicemail again.

Maria asked Katie if she wanted to go to work with her. Katie reached for her mom's hand; nothing else had to be said. As she drove to the restaurant, Katie safely with her, Maria mentally put on her work hat.

Her uncle was standing in front of the building when they arrived, arguing with a food supplier she recognized. Before opening the car door, she told Katie this was going to be a hard day at the restaurant, as something troubling had happened with taxes.

Katie wanted to ask what taxes were, but by the look on her mom's face and the argument her uncle was having, she knew now wasn't the time. She would save her questions.

Katie sat in the corner, away from the fray, and opened her backpack.

She removed her library book and, page by page, put the book back together. She began reading it, oblivious to the chaos around her.

Joan of Arc, she read, was from a peasant family in France. She learned how to sew and clean from her mother, but she dreamed of being a great leader fighting battles to help her country. After working very hard to build an army that trusted her—just like George Washington, Katie figured—the king gave her a horse and weapons. She was brave and led France against England, winning a great battle. Later she was captured and, to Katie's shock, was burned at the stake. Then she read at the end of the book that the Catholic Pope made Joan of Arc a saint because of her bravery and success.

She closed the book and began to study the cover. It depicted a young woman on a white horse, wearing a metal shield, holding a shiny silver sword.

Her trance was broken by the crashing sound of a large metal pot bouncing off a wall, hitting the floor. Her mom walked over to her aunt, not knowing what to say.

Katie heard her aunt say, "They've taken every dollar out of our account, and all the checks we wrote to suppliers have bounced, along with our rent check, Maria. The bank just confirmed it." She was sobbing. "The suppliers are picking up their food; we can't even open today."

Maria knew in her heart that this didn't have to happen. If only her aunt and uncle had let her help run the business, instead of spending most of her time cooking and cleaning. Though she was sad for them, this outcome reinforced to her that she could run a successful restaurant. She could do it—if only she had capital to get started.

Just then her phone rang. It was Tony.

He arrived at the chaos twenty minutes later. Katie was still sitting at the corner table, now coloring a picture of a horse, adding her interpretation with a sparkly red-and-yellow tail. Tony hugged Maria and her aunt and uncle, and then sat next to Katie. His normal calm demeanor, which both Maria and Katie had come to rely upon, was different today. Instead, he seemed agitated, almost angry. With intense eyes, he looked at Katie and asked her who the girls were that hurt her.

"Daddy, I don't know their names. The school is going to find out. What's wrong? You're scaring me."

Tony had never been so angry. Someone hurting his child, pushing her to the ground, even kicking her . . . the more he thought of it, the more enraged he became. He had sacrificed for a better life for his family, his father had been murdered for it, and now someone had attacked his daughter. This could not go unpunished.

Though Maria tried to stop him, to calm him, he hopped in his truck, gunned it, and headed for Katie's school. Maria and Katie were close behind. Their hearts raced. When they arrived, Tony was already in the school office, and they could hear his voice booming through the closed doors as they approached.

The school secretary was doing the best job she could, explaining to him that she wasn't able to give the suspected girls' names, and that the principal would be contacting him tomorrow about what they would do. Tony wasn't having it. He pounded his fist on her desk as the police pulled up. Maria was tugging him backward, away from the frightened secretary's desk, as the two officers entered. They wrestled Tony to the floor and cuffed him while Katie watched, frozen, unable to make a sound.

Tony didn't resist the officers. The metallic click of cuffs closing around his wrists hit like a bucket of ice water. *What the hell have I done?* He sat on the floor, trying to catch his breath, dizzy from the thunderous sound of his own heartbeat. He didn't look up, afraid of making eye contact with his wife or daughter. Shame was an emotion new to him, one he now understood was far worse than any punch in the gut.

Officer Osgood took statements from the school secretary and Maria, glancing over at Tony as he wrote the report. Katie stood and raised the back of her shirt to show the bruise which had turned dark purple, the size of a baseball, and with tears in her eyes showed them her ripped-up library book. The prodigious eight-year-old looked up at the officer and recognized what she hoped for: an almost imperceptible look of sympathy that emerged when he glanced again at her father. The officer shut his report book as the other helped Tony to his feet, and they escorted him to the backseat of their police car, with Maria and Katie close behind.

Officer Osgood explained where Tony would be taken for processing and suggested they contact an attorney. He handed Maria a business card with a report number on it and shared, loudly enough for Tony to hear, that they would follow up regarding the assault on her daughter. "We will investigate what happened to your daughter; you can depend upon that," he assured them.

Maria and Katie quickly went home, found Betty Lam's business card, and called her. Maria relayed the emergency nature of her call to her assistant and was told she was with another client but would contact them soon. Bella was hanging on every word that streamed from Katie while Maria was on the phone.

When she hung up, the three sat at the kitchen table, silent, staring at the phone. A few minutes later, the sound of the ring jolted them back to the moment, and Maria nearly knocked the phone from the table trying to answer. Betty Lam was on the other end, her voice calm as she began asking rapid-fire questions. Ten minutes later, she explained she wasn't a criminal attorney, but two doors down the hall from her she knew someone with an excellent reputation who specialized in criminal law. She added he was a Rotarian friend of hers and asked Maria if she wanted to speak with him.

Maria didn't know what a Rotarian was, but it sounded significant, and she trusted Betty so she agreed gratefully. As Maria hung up the phone, the three most important people in Tony's life—his wife, mother, and daughter—sat around the table talking, reliving every detail of the last hour, somehow gaining strength and hope from one another.

Betty walked down the hall to the office of Matt Lucas, a trusted friend and colleague. She peered through his window to see no one sitting in front of him. He was leaning back in his chair with his feet on the desk, immersed in a file he had open. As she lightly knocked on his door he looked up, smiled, and motioned her in. Betty asked if he had a few minutes. He did for her, he said, and she filled him in on Tony and his family—decent, hardworking people, she said. Her concern was not only the criminal issue but how it would affect Tony's immigration status. She was worried this might derail his chance to become legal, including potentially being deported.

Matt thought about it for roughly thirty seconds. Known for a razor-sharp legal mind and a soft spot for the underdog, he told himself even if it was pro bono, he could wrap it up quickly. And it would be a welcome relief from the arrogant scumbag he was defending now, who was definitely not pro bono.

Maria, still sitting next to the phone, jumped as it rang.

"Mrs. Gonzales, this is Matt Lucas. Your attorney, Betty Lam, asked me to give you a call. I understand your husband needs my help."

He asked her several more questions, including whether Tony had ever been in trouble with the law before. As he hung up, he looked over the two pages of notes he'd written. This one had a chance for easy resolution, he hoped. From what Betty had told him about the family, and the fact that he didn't touch the school secretary, didn't resist arrest—all of it boded well for him.

As Matt pulled into a plum parking spot across from the always teeming three-story county jail, he flinched at the sight of a full-size nondescript bus parked close to an exit. He'd seen it before. It belonged to ICE—Immigration and Customs Enforcement—not a good sign for his new client. He showed his ID to the guard at the front entry, walked through the metal detector, and signed in with another correctional officer, arranging to have his client brought to a meeting room. At the end of a long, dingy hall was where attorneys met with clients to plot a way out of the system. Most of the time, it was an exercise in futility. Matt's batting average was better than most.

Correctional Officer Larry Formentera gave a nod to Matt as he unlocked the small, dimly lit concrete room. Matt had known him for years, often coming to the jail several times per week to meet with his various clients. Larry had always been friendly.

"Saw the ICE limo outside today. Are they handpicking or doing a sweep?" Matt asked nonchalantly.

"Looks like the limo will be full, Mr. Lucas. Don't think they'll be headed to Napa Valley for wine tasting, though." He chuckled, leaving Matt to get settled in the folding chair.

Ten minutes later, already in an orange jumpsuit, a terrified Tony Gonzales was brought in. Matt introduced himself and explained that he had spoken with and been retained by Maria, through the contact of his colleague, Betty Lam. Tony looked relieved—a look Matt had seen before. He said, "Let's get down to business, Tony. They don't give us much time."

Over the next twenty minutes, Matt took copious notes. He learned from Tony's recollection how and why the event at the school took place, and he confirmed that there had been no contact with the school secretary and he didn't resist arrest. He hoped the police report would corroborate his account. Matt made a note to have Maria take pictures of the child's bruised back today.

Unfortunately, he also confirmed that an agent from ICE had spoken with him a short time before, along with several other men in holding. Matt knew this was going to complicate Tony's path.

—⁓—

Tony gazed out the window of the urine-smelling ICE bus as they crossed the Carquinez Bridge. The waterway led to the San Francisco Bay with a mountainous backdrop. On any other day it would have seemed beautiful to Tony. He was grateful, though. Matt had explained in relative terms what would be happening, where he would be going, and what the process would be to hopefully get him home. Thanks to Maria, he had a good attorney. Thanks to his mother, he had his attorney fees covered for what was now two attorneys, one for the criminal part and the other for the immigration part. As he looked around the crowded bus, he doubted many of the other detainees had the backup he did . . . and yet, here he was.

Katie had asked him about trust. He had tried to answer her question thoughtfully, with the authority of an elder. But what did he know about trust? How, indeed, do you know when you can and can't trust someone? Sometimes, it seemed, your only option was to trust someone. It was your only hope.

It had been almost a month since Katie had seen her father. Each day she wrote him a letter, telling him about the Es for excellence she was receiving in school, about her grandmother's garden, about the books she was reading. By her bed, she had hung a wall calendar, and before she went to sleep each night, she drew a little heart for him on that day.

She'd drawn a lot of hearts. Today she was excited that she, her mother, and her grandmother were driving to the detention center to see him. She knew he didn't want her to see him there, but she couldn't wait any longer. Katie had to see her daddy.

The gravel parking lot was huge. Maria finally found a space not too far from the entrance to the detention center. Even the massive structure, itself surrounded by rolls of barbed wire atop twelve-foot slatted metal fencing, felt foreboding and gloomy.

Maria pulled the keys from the ignition and looked over at Bella and Katie. Neither moved as they absorbed the scene. After a few moments, Maria softly asked, "Well, this is where your dad is, Katie. Are you sure you want to go in?"

Her head flooded with questions for her mother. "Why is he here? Is he with really bad people? Will he get to come home?" But instead she opened her car door and only said, "Come on, Grandma, Daddy needs us." Bella followed, pushing her walker over the uneven gravel.

—⁓—

The months that followed were exhausting and frustrating to the Gonzales family, punctuated with occasional steps forward. Tony's charges had been dropped by the district attorney, thanks to an obliging police report and the thoroughness of attorney Matt Lucas. They all thought that would lead to his immediate release from the

ICE detention center. Katie had attended most of Maria's meetings with the two attorneys. Each time she sat next to her mother, silently assessing if they could be trusted. Her dad had been in detention for a long time.

Betty was frustrated too. She'd completed and filed all the pertinent paperwork on time. The t's were crossed and the i's were dotted. Still the decision lingered. Unfortunately, she knew ICE marched to their own drummer, and she thought it was as much about numbers, quotas, and politics as anything. And, of course, Tony had entered the U.S. illegally.

Then, one Monday morning, Maria got the call from Betty they had been waiting for.

As Betty, Maria, Katie, and Bella stood at the gate of the detention center, Katie holding both Betty's and Maria's hands, they each felt grateful and elated. Unlike most of his fellow detainees, some of whom truly were bad characters, Tony was coming home to his family.

Hugs, tears, and more hugs greeted him. Once back in her Lexus SUV, Betty chortled, "Everyone's seatbelt on? We're not giving ICE *any* chance to change their minds. Let's get the hell out of here."

They all cheered. Katie now had another hero in Betty, like Joan of Arc from her book. Betty gave the credit to colleague Matt Lucas, without whom, she said, this day would not have come. Katie thought, *Two people we can trust . . . just like Daddy said, "When things are tough, make sure you have people you trust standing by your side."*

As they pulled into Fairfield, Tony felt overwhelming emotion. He was *home* with his family, safe again. Bella couldn't contain her elation any longer. Not only was her son home, but she had—they all had—a big surprise for him.

Downtown Fairfield, the SUV pulled to the curb. Bella motioned for Tony to look out the window. There, atop the restaurant that Tony thought had been closed for good, stood a large, colorful sign.

He read *Bella's Mexican Cuisine*. Katie had named their already popular restaurant.

FIVE

Schools were set to reopen after a two-week holiday on January 3rd, so most students and workers were enjoying a last day before the real world kicked back in and they returned to a routine. Today, however—January 2, 2012—felt extra special to three young people: Leon, Taylor, and Katie. They were officially becoming teenagers. It was their thirteenth birthday.

—⁓—

Katie awoke to the sound of a book hitting her hardwood floor. Most nights she fell asleep reading, lately about the Civil War. She stretched her arms and looked out her window as she smiled . . . today was her birthday.

Gazing at the friendship bracelet on her wrist, Katie pulled the covers up tightly under her chin, cuddling with her threadbare stuffed owl. The owl, won in a library read-a-thon a few years before, when she was just a kid, was her favorite stuffed animal among the many that adorned her cheery bedroom. The bracelet was new.

Katie was nearly as tall as her mother, with medium-length, wavy dark hair she chose to wear pulled back in a ponytail most days. Her black-framed glasses were a recent addition, ones she carefully selected for herself when the eye doctor determined her headaches were due to a combination of excessive reading and poor eyesight. Some of her older classmates accused her of looking "geeky" with her glasses, but she didn't care. They gave her a new sense of confidence, and her headaches went away. And Luke Nobili, the fourteen-year-old boy who had given her the friendship bracelet, said he thought she looked nice in them.

Most thirteen-year-olds were in eighth grade, but Katie had skipped two grades. Tony and Maria were reluctant to allow the early move to high school, but when her off-the-charts test scores were confirmed and the unique accelerated learning program at Armijo High School was explained to the family, all agreed it was the best decision for Katie's academic future. Betty Lam, now a close family friend as well as their immigration attorney, weighed in on the decision, as did Mrs. Stone, Katie's favorite librarian. Both felt certain she could handle the work.

Katie had not been afraid, only excited for the new challenge. Now, with her second semester of high school upon her, she'd made friends, and for the first time, she felt like she fit in. And also for the first time, her schoolwork was a challenge, one that she relished.

Katie lay in bed thinking she was happy with her life—with one caveat. She needed to convince her parents that working in the family's restaurant every day after school was not for her. She needed the time to study, and she wanted to join Interact, a club on campus where she could have fun helping people. But those thoughts were for another day; today was her birthday. She put her owl carefully on the bookcase where he lived, made her bed, and headed toward the aroma of fresh tortillas, eggs, and chorizo. Grandma Bella was making her a breakfast feast.

Tony and Maria took the day off so they could spend it with their daughter. Closing the restaurant for two days in a row was rare for them, but spending Katie's birthday with her was worth everything. So, with the kitchen filled with a smell that made their mouths water, Bella brought the scrumptious-looking plates to the table. As she sat to join the happy trio, their family felt complete. They all dug in.

The day's game plan included a family trip to the Oakland Zoo, one of Katie's favorite things to do growing up, followed by her first "friend party." Her dad raised an eyebrow when he heard both girls and boys were invited. Her mom just smiled. Maria convinced him that pizza and video games at Scandia Amusement Park was nothing to worry about. She hadn't told him yet that they were picking up a boy named Luke to go to the zoo with them.

"Daddy, he's not my boyfriend. He's just my friend. We sit next to each other in classes."

Tony was silent as his one-year-old Chevy pickup headed toward the rural area outside of the town he knew so well. They were all silent, in fact. Maria looked at Katie, sitting in the backseat with her arms folded across her chest. She gave her a quick wink. Katie hastened to add, with certainty in her voice, "And, Daddy, you will like him. He has manners, and he wants to be a vet. Oh, and he's a really good soccer player."

Tony had softened, but he still wasn't convinced as they pulled up to Luke's house.

Under a clear blue sky, a crisp California sixty degrees, Luke's younger brother and sister played catch in the front yard. His sister, Khloe, ran to the front door to summon Luke. His brother, Gabe, walked up to the pickup to say hi, trying not to be obvious as he glanced at Katie. *Yes*, he thought, *she really is pretty*. Shannon, their mom, came out to greet the family and thanked them warmly for bringing her son with them to the zoo. She said it was one of his favorite places to go.

Luke came out the front door, waving as he jogged to the pickup.

Smartly dressed in a soccer sweatshirt and Nike shoes, hair neatly cut, with a look of uncertainty, he reached out his hand to Tony and thanked all of them for bringing him along. "I'm Luke, sir," he said as he hopped in the backseat with Grandma Bella firmly between the teenagers. Leaning over so Katie could see him, he wished her happy birthday and asked which animals she liked most. During the forty-five minutes to the zoo, they talked nonstop about school, soccer, and who was coming to her birthday party at Scandia that evening.

Tony and Maria grinned at each other in the front seat. Maria whispered, "It's official. We have a teenager." Tony shook his head, clearly more relaxed.

—⁓—

Leon was up early that morning. Grandma made him his favorite breakfast of oatmeal, bacon, and orange juice. She and his dad, John, had decorated the table with Happy Birthday décor, including birthday plates and a three-inch bright red button he could pin on his shirt with the words *Hug me, it's my 13th birthday!* As he smiled at their effort, he vowed not to wear it outside the house. He was a teenager. He wasn't going to risk running into one of his asshole classmates with that button on. They didn't need any extra fodder against him.

He was used to the red hair jokes, the teasing about being skinny, and the subtle pushes when teachers were around—which were not as subtle in their absence. As he sat at the table, enjoying his breakfast, pretending not to appreciate the kiss on top of his head from Grandma, Leon recalled his last day of school before Christmas break.

Alone, as was his typical preference, Leon was in the gym early before school started, practicing free throws. His eighth-grade basketball coach and math teacher, Coach Litner, had an office just outside the gym. He'd grown accustomed each morning to hearing the sound of Leon's basketball pounding the hardwood and swishing through the net. Sitting in his office, the coach never heard a word spoken, only the relentless sound of the solitary basketball. Sometimes, and he didn't understand why, the hair on the back of his neck would stand up, followed by a shudder. A quick glance into the gym always assured him that it was just Leon, not a ghost, playing basketball.

Leon had become a remarkable free-throw shooter for his age, hitting nearly 80 percent in practice. The coach often praised him for his work ethic and focus in front of the team at after-school practice. Leon would try not to smile, but he couldn't help it. Even with his solid ball handling skills, he hadn't earned a place on the A team. His problem, as Coach saw it, was lack of confidence in a real game. Though he was one of the tallest on the floor, his slight build allowed others, including players from his own team, to knock him off his feet. Coach Litner had drills in practice specifically to help a few of his boys work on their footwork and stability. He was pleased to see the progress Leon made and expected that he would be on the A team before the season was over.

Sitting at his desk, the coach was immersed in grading over a hundred math tests. Sipping his high-octane Dutch Bros. coffee was helping him keep his pace. The goal was to finish all of his paperwork that day so he could leave for Christmas vacation with nothing hanging over him.

The almost hypnotic sound of Leon's basketball in the background became white noise as Coach Litner plowed through his task. But when he heard voices and the sound of the basketball stopped, his honed middle school teacher–antennae alerted him to pay attention.

"You think you're so great, making shots all by yourself!" he heard someone say. "You're just a pimple-faced loser. We're tired of you kissing up to Coach. Why don't you just quit and make everyone happy!" Three boys were shouting. Their harangue was gaining momentum.

As Coach turned the corner and entered the gym, he heard them add, "And *everyone* knows your mother is in prison! You're a loser, just like her."

What he saw next, in the few seconds it took him to reach the scene beneath the hoop, he would always remember in vivid detail. Tears were rolling down Leon's face as he metamorphosed before the coach's eyes, turning from punching bag to aggressor. A kick to the chest sent one boy flying, and a windmill of fists brought on not one, but two, bloody noses. The perpetrators made no effort to fight back.

Leon looked up at Coach Litner, both of them shocked at what had happened. "I'm sorry, Coach, they just pushed me too far this time" was all he said, probably the most words Coach had ever heard him say at one time.

All four boys were suspended from school for two days, so their vacation was extended. The principal made a mental note that next semester would include schoolwide lessons on bullying. It wasn't the first time she'd seen students confronted by this cruelty, and sadly, she understood, it wouldn't be the last. Current research was conclusive— the experience of being bullied had a lasting impact on a child.

The unending and complicated job of trying to teach compassion felt unachievable today. She was thankful tomorrow was the start of Christmas vacation.

At Leon's breakfast table, along with his specially prepared birthday breakfast, John had placed a hastily wrapped elongated gift. He had placed two mismatched bows on the top, his way of showing the importance of this gift, and with a big smile he pushed it toward Leon.

"Dad, can I open it now?" Leon asked, already beginning to rip away the Spiderman wrapping paper. The box had a picture of a young man holding a shotgun at his shoulder, looking down the barrel with his finger on the trigger—the Winchester SXP Trap twelve-gauge.

John was as excited as Leon. He went on about the satin finish, the thirty-inch barrel, lightweight, three-shot adapter, and fiber optics—a perfect starter gun for trap shooting. Grandma had recently added the equipment and layout for trap shooting in back of the gun range, already generating twenty-one new members. Leon was over the moon. What a birthday, and he still had a laser tag party tonight at Scandia Amusement Park.

John suggested they put his SXP together and give it a whirl—with no complaints from his delighted son. They opened the box and laid out all the parts with the instructions. Piece by piece, it took shape. The stock was walnut, the long barrel cool to the touch and perfectly smooth.

Leon loved this shotgun, his first real gun. Until now, his often-used Daisy BB gun was his favorite, responsible for annihilating most of the population of lizards and squirrels at their small ranch. He even tried shooting a skunk one time, and only one time, with the Daisy. He remembered, a week later, after numerous rain showers, the slight vindication he'd felt upon finding its dead carcass a few hundred feet away.

The afternoon was cloudy and cool, perfect for shooting clay targets. Father and son took turns, with Grandma working their MEC Clay Target Launcher. The entire supply of 240 sporting clays on hand that day were blown to bits, with Leon getting his fair share.

John patted him on the back. "Nice job, son. You're going to be a marksman."

Leon felt sure his dad was right.

Leon's best friend, really his only friend, was a girl named Mendy. They had been in the same classes for a few years and shared many of the same interests, among them basketball and video games. Mendy would save a seat next to her at lunch for Leon, and no matter who, by happenstance, would attempt to sit there, she'd shoo them away. After a while, no one tried anymore, and they ate in peace. Sometimes they'd talk a little about schoolwork, a video game, or why she limped some days, but most of the time they'd sit quietly and eat their lunches, content to have a friend. A rough game of basketball followed, Mendy usually with the high score, which suited Leon just fine.

The country school they attended had a chicken coop and raised rabbits so the students could participate in caring for them. Mendy liked feeding the chickens and gathering the eggs, and she took pride in raking the coop so it was clean. Leon differed. He often asked her, "What's the point? Why do they matter to you? They're just going to be chicken nuggets anyway." She didn't have an answer for him, but to her they mattered. And so she kept the commitment to her teacher and arrived early each morning before school.

Early in the week, Grandma asked him who he'd like to invite to his "Big Thirteen" birthday party. He didn't hesitate: Mendy. Besides family, that was it. Grandma and John looked at each other, surprised with his choice and more than a little intrigued to meet her. Scandia laser tag reservations were made for two, pizza was ordered, and a table secured for four at 6:00 p.m. to celebrate.

—⁓—

Taylor had a big decision to make, and he didn't want to think about it anymore. It was still fairly dark, as he cuddled with his soft pillow, trying to get comfortable after a night of tossing and turning. His football posters on the far wall were now distinguishable, so he knew sunrise wasn't far away. He covered up his head with the clean-smelling sheet in the hope that he could go back to sleep.

A tap on the door stirred him. His room was awash in sunlight, and he was surprised by the confirmation of his iPhone: he'd slept in to 9:10. The door opened to Taylor's mom and dad singing a slightly off-key but enthusiastic "Happy Birthday."

He'd forgotten, with all the worry, that it was his thirteenth birthday. "Hey, sleepyhead," Tom prodded. "Mom's making your favorite breakfast. How about you come downstairs and join us before it gets cold?"

Taylor smiled as he stretched his long arms and said, "Be there in five, Dad, and don't eat my bacon!"

Along with cheesy scrambled eggs with chives and crispy bacon, Jenny, his foster mom—he just called her "Mom"—had prepared homemade cinnamon rolls. The aroma of bacon coupled with cinnamon had Taylor skipping steps on the way down the stairs. Sitting on the table was a beautifully wrapped present with a blue metallic bow that looked like a fireworks explosion. There was a sealed envelope next to it with his mom's decorative handwriting—"Happy Birthday, Taylor."

He wanted to be happy this morning. It was his birthday. He had his favorite breakfast, the most beautiful present he'd ever seen, and it was all for him. The people at this table loved him, and he loved them right back. *What is wrong with me?* he wondered. This should be an easy decision . . . but it was complicated, even for a thirteen-year-old.

Enough, he told himself, and lifted a thick piece of bacon, cooked crispy, just the way he liked it.

Tom, recently retired for the second time as fire chief at Suisun City, had been watching Taylor intently. His heart ached for him, feeling to his core that the decision imposed upon this child, now a teenager, was unfair and just plain cruel. It had all started with a call a few months back, from the same social worker who brought Taylor to them a short five years before.

Cynthia Garcia had made many visits to their home over the last several years. This was one of her success stories, maybe her most successful pairing. The memory of standing in front of Tom and Jenny's red front door, seeing the connection unfold in those few short moments their eyes met, was what kept her going in the tough times of her job. It gave her hope for other children, trying always to find that "right match."

So when Taylor's father contacted her and asked for her help to find and ultimately gain back custody of his son, she was stunned. Before alerting Tom and Jenny, or certainly Taylor, she wanted to do a thorough background check and get a clear picture of Michael Turner. She found out Michael had been convicted of second-degree murder, thirteen years ago and had been released several years early for good behavior.

Michael had been residing in a halfway house in Rio Vista, a sleepy town fifteen miles outside of Fairfield. Adjacent to the Sacramento River, Rio Vista's claim to fame was a massive drawbridge and a large number of boat docks for all sizes and values of personal watercraft. He landed a job as an apprentice in a thriving boat repair business, where he worked hard to earn the trust of the owner. Somehow, despite the twelve miserable years he'd wasted in prison, losing the woman he loved, and not being there to raise his child, Michael retained a sliver of hope that life could still bestow some happiness. He liked the hard work; he just needed a little luck this time. And he needed his son.

The thorough background check completed, Cynthia met with Michael again. His preparation to be responsible parent was compelling. He'd found a clean two-bedroom apartment close to his work and a few blocks from the local middle school. He passed two drug tests, and his boss at work had high praise for his dependability and work ethic. Cynthia couldn't help but be impressed by his determination—and she had no choice. The law was clear about parental rights taking precedence if a parent was deemed able to provide a safe, healthy environment.

This is where the discretion of the social worker came into play. Sadly, it was not an exact science.

Tom said he would explain things in a few days to Taylor, after Thanksgiving. Jenny sobbed quietly into her pillow that night, trying not to let Taylor hear her despair. She was at risk of losing her son and couldn't bear it. Tom went for a drive after dinner, returning after Taylor's lights were out and only Jenny's bedside lamp was on. When he entered their bedroom, she was still awake, though, and could see that his eyes were puffy.

———

In early December, Tom and Taylor sat next to each other in the waiting area of Social Services, trying to take their minds off Taylor's impending first meeting with his biological father. As his foot tapped incessantly, he read through the war-torn October edition of *Sports Illustrated*. It had articles about several of Taylor's favorite NFL players. He'd been hoping for a comeback by his team, the Eagles, but they had sunk to the dismal record of 4–10. He toyed with the idea of switching favorite teams, but his dad was a die-hard Philadelphia fan, through good years and bad. If they were his dad's favorite, then they were his too. Besides, he had a genuine signed poster by LeSean McCoy, the Eagles running back, on his wall, compliments of his dad.

Cynthia opened the door leading to the waiting room, holding her notebook against her chest, and quickly found Tom and Taylor. As she approached, Taylor looked up from his magazine, which had served its purpose that day. He noticed a pin on the lapel of her jacket, just like the one his dad wore.

Tom stood and gave Cynthia a hug. "How's my favorite Rotary buddy? Nice sitting next to you yesterday—great meeting, by the way."

She perked up and chuckled, "What about that president of ours? Jerry Wilkerson was on fire yesterday. That was the first time I was ever put on time out for disturbing the peace. And then he fined me five dollars! Wait until I'm sergeant next time."

The strain on their faces had evaporated. Cynthia sat next to Taylor and explained in her compassionate but confident voice what would be happening today. "You'll be meeting your biological father in a few minutes, Taylor. I'll be there with you along with your therapist. Your dad will wait here for you. It will last up to an hour. You'll have lots of time to ask questions and get to know your father a little bit. Nothing will be decided today, Taylor, and ultimately you will make the decision. Before we go in, do you have any questions for me?"

Looking shell-shocked, he could only shake his head.

They all stood. Feeling helpless and empty, Tom watched Taylor and Cynthia disappear through the self-locking door.

Taylor and Cynthia went into a little room with a metal table and a couple of wooden chairs. It looked to Taylor like an interrogation room from a TV show. In one of the chairs, looking him in the face, was a stranger—his father.

"Taylor," the man said, standing.

Taylor didn't respond.

His father laughed. "Come here," he said.

Taylor looked at Cynthia. She nodded. She'd told him before that she didn't have to hug his father if he didn't want to. He didn't have to do anything he didn't want to.

Taylor turned and approached to give his father a brief, awkward hug. He sat down, feeling numb.

His father sat too. "How are you?" he asked his son.

"Okay," Taylor said.

"Okay? That's it?"

"I'm good."

His father laughed again. Taylor looked at Cynthia. She wasn't smiling. She looked tense.

"It's all right," said Taylor's father, leaning back in his chair. "I'm glad to finally meet you."

An awkward silence ensued. Taylor sat frozen in his chair.

The forced smile returned to Michael's face. "You're a big, strong kid. Are you playing any sports? Going out for football?"

Taylor shifted in his chair. A smile flitted across his face. He said, "I want to."

"You want to. Are you going to?"

"Uh," said Taylor. He looked at Cynthia. Then, for the first time, he looked up again and made eye contact with his father. "Concussions are kind of a big deal, right?"

Michael laughed loudly. "Sure they are. That's why you don't use your head like a battering ram. Plus you don't want to break your neck.

You've got to use your shoulders. Here."

He stood, then, and motioned for Taylor to stand.

Taylor stood, trying not to grin. His father walked him through the proper way to tackle someone. "You won't be having to face down somebody as big as me," he said, "but this will work every time you're on that field."

Cynthia watched, uncertain. It was a little soon for demonstrations of physical activity. But this was the boy's father.

And when they took their seats again, something had changed. They'd settled into something, a kind of comfort.

Taylor opened up. When his father asked him about school, he volunteered how well he was doing in science. By the time the meeting ended, Taylor's father had brought his son fully out of his shell. They laughed together about something—some movie they had both seen. Cynthia hadn't heard of it.

Other meetings followed. The bond between them only got stronger. Before long, the thirteen years of separation had vanished. Cynthia was always there at the meetings, now called "visits," but she receded more and more into the background. Before long, it was as if she wasn't even there.

They talked about everything, even about his mom, Maggie. Michael told Taylor how proud of him she would be. He explained how they'd met and that he thought about her every day, her strength, honesty, and determination to be a good mother, a good person. He told him how his mother had made him into a better man, how her memory helped him survive in prison, knowing someday he'd prove it to her, to Taylor. Through the last few visits, Cynthia told them she saw her role as the supplier of tissues, and they all had a good laugh. She'd used her fair share of the Kleenex box, too.

At home, Taylor opened up a little bit about his father, though Tom and Jenny were careful not to pry. He volunteered, almost defensively, at dinner one night, that his father had been falsely convicted of shooting someone and that was why he'd gone to prison. They simply didn't know how to respond, so they just listened. Their happy-go-lucky Taylor was reserved with them in a way he'd never been. He was pulling away.

Somehow the taste and crunch of crispy bacon, and the realization he was the center of his parents' universe, enveloped Taylor. On this birthday morning, for the first time in weeks, he knew he'd be okay. Whatever decision he made, whether to stay with the Arthurs or move with his biological father, it would work out. A tear trickled down his cheek as the relief sank in. Yes, he'd be all right. Without warning, he reached out to his mom and hugged her tightly, the kind of hug moms don't forget. Tom watched, overcome with emotion. "Dad, I love you," said Taylor, clearly choked up as he gave his dad a bear hug.

The three were all smiles and sniffs, the table covered with birthday napkins, crumpled and moist with tears. They finished breakfast with talk about football and their successful Rotary Bell-ringing challenge for the Salvation Army on Christmas Eve. Together, Taylor and his dad had rung the red kettle bell in front of Walmart, collecting a record-setting $1,018 in two hours.

His mom could barely contain herself as she pushed the handsomely wrapped present in front of Taylor. He grabbed for his cell and took a couple of pictures to put on Facebook before ripping off the bow. He'd been eyeing the tantalizing package, trying to guess what might be inside. He'd concluded it was too big for a basketball or football, but not big enough to be a TV for his room. He was ready to find out. Three seconds later, with clapping from his parents, he opened a nondescript box. In it was another box. This one bore a picture of an iPad!

Even though he was officially a teenager now, he couldn't help jumping up and down and screaming. He hadn't dared to ask for one, but he was thrilled. Beneath the iPad was something else . . . the eyes of his parents were focused squarely on him in anticipation. As he unwrapped a second gift, this one in layers of neat white tissue paper, he saw a scrapbook. On the front was a photo of Taylor between his mom and dad at the Bodega Bay Beach. He was proudly holding up a starfish.

Taylor gingerly opened the book. He scanned page after page of photos that chronicled his last five years. Each page was artfully penned, with a description and date of when and where . . . he didn't need it, though. Each image was already ingrained in his memory.

He knew he'd been given a gift of immeasurable significance. His mom and dad, though sometimes annoying, and even embarrassing, in the eyes of a preteen, proved their love for him many times over. He closed the book, the first time of perhaps a thousand to follow. He couldn't speak. Tom and Jenny thought they could see, could feel, what it meant to him, but it only scratched the surface. This scrapbook would be one of a handful of his life's treasures he'd have until the end.

———

Michael Turner had saved some money and planned something special for the evening of his son's birthday. It was the first time they were going somewhere unaccompanied by Cynthia—Taylor's guardian angel, as Tom called her. Michael had asked his boss if he could borrow the company pickup to take Taylor out for his thirteenth birthday, and they'd even talked about ideas of where to go, a place he hadn't been since he was kid: Scandia Amusement Park. Michael's boss said they had taken their grandson there to play something called laser tag, followed by pizza and video games. It had been a good time for all.

Michael and Taylor arrived just as the first downpour began, easily finding a parking spot close to the entrance. They hustled to the entry doors, both trying to open the door for the other, as rain pounded on them. They were laughing as Michael said, "After you, son." It was the first time he'd called Taylor "son." *Feeling comfortable with each other takes time*, Michael thought. He was enjoying every minute.

The noise level in the video arcade was intense. As they walked down the aisles on the way to the pizza restaurant, one aisle was by far the busiest, with kids standing three-deep, watching and cheering. Michael noticed the names atop these popular games were *Kill Shot* and *Thud*. As he and Taylor slowed to see what was causing the cheering, he was stunned. There on the screen was a character chasing down terrified people on a street, shooting them in the back of the head as the points rolled on.

With each kill shot, the group roared. Michael was no stranger to violence, but this was too much even for him, and he didn't want his son to see any more of it.

Most of the tables had "Reserved" signs on them, but they were still able to find an empty one. As they looked at the pizza menu, father and son realized another "first" was about to happen—what each considered their favorite pizza. Taylor was quick to defer to his father's favorite, but Michael said, "It's your birthday; you get to pick, no arguing," with a big smile on his face. Taylor ordered the Hawaiian-style pie with Canadian bacon and pineapple. And it became Michael's favorite too.

Laser tag was scheduled for 7:00 p.m., and the check-in lady said it was now full. With the addition of Taylor, all twenty-five slots were reserved. Anything with guns, even toy laser guns, gave Michael anxiety, so he opted to sit in the waiting area until the tag game was over. Taylor suited up with a vest and a fully charged laser gun.

At six that evening, Katie's family and her friend, Luke, pulled into the packed parking lot of Scandia. Bella had decided, on the way back, to sit by a window so the friends could sit next to each other, but she remained vigilant. After all, Katie was her granddaughter. She admitted to herself they were sort of cute together, both of them talking all of the way back from the zoo about the personalities of orangutans, the sizable herd of elephants, and other observations of the day. It had been chilly, but only on the drive to Scandia, it had begun to drizzle. The weather report indicated the potential of thunder and lightning, a rare occurrence in Fairfield. Several friends from school had RSVP'd to attend, and Maria had reserved a room for the party with balloons, pizza, and cake.

Katie greeted her friends as they arrived. An array of pizzas was brought in, something for every taste. Bella leaned on her cane as she made her way around the table of twelve, making sure all the guests had food and drink. There was an Asian boy with a short haircut, a tall blonde girl with a ponytail and thick glasses, an African-American boy in khakis and a starched shirt, and a short, slightly pudgy boy with freckles. All looked smart and were friends of her Katie. Bella had learned to admire more and more about America, where so many cultures came together and learned from each other—most of the time, anyway.

Pizza finished, it was nearing 7:00 pm. "Time for laser tag!" Tony announced.

Katie, Luke, and their friends headed toward check-in. For most, it was their first laser tag experience, and they were anxious to get a full set of instructions.

—⁓—

Having trouble finding a close parking place in the rain, Leon's dad slowly perused the parking lot outside Scandia. Finally, a dark Nissan SUV backed out, and John's trusty pickup claimed the spot. Grandma doled out umbrellas, but Leon declined, preferring to run for it with his hood up. As he opened the heavy glass door, the sounds of a hundred video games poured out. The bells, dings, pings, and screeches made the adrenaline flow for the thirteen-year-old. Leon's eyes searched the entry for his friend, Mendy. She wasn't there yet, but he recognized a couple of the boys from basketball who had attacked him playing *Mortal Enemy* near the entry. He smiled at the memory of kicking their butts. It was something worth being suspended over.

Just then, Mendy walked through the door. He ran over and gave her a hug. She flinched, an ingrained reaction to someone coming close. Leon thought he understood and didn't want to embarrass her, so just said he was glad she came. And he was. Her worn tennis shoes were drenched, far beyond what a short walk from the parking lot would have done. But she thought that, for the feeling of being valued, it was worth the miles she'd walked, even if much of it had been in the rain.

Leon led her to their reserved table, where John and Grandma welcomed her. Hot pepperoni pizza had just been dropped off, with a green salad and pitcher of root beer. John poured a round in the plastic cups, and they all toasted Leon on his thirteenth birthday, and then dished up pizza and salad. Even Leon was talkative as they ate. He shared about his present, the shotgun. Mendy talked about her chickens at school, avoiding any reference to her home life.

Grandma could see Mendy was eyeing the leftover pizza, and without asking if she wanted more, she nonchalantly put the biggest piece on her empty plate, saying, "Let's not waste this delicious pizza. Everyone eat up."

Not a slice of pizza left, the four headed over for Leon and Mendy to check in for laser tag. While they walked, he was animated, confident as he told Mendy he'd played three times before and it was super fun. Explaining the game to her, he had no idea there would be a slightly different version for his fourth experience.

——

The sound of thunder could be heard even above the video games. The last few players were arriving, some wet, as the clock neared the seven o'clock start for the epic laser tag session. Seasoned veteran players knew that the secret to winning the game was being the first players in the door to get set up quickly. Then as the rest of the players entered, they could run up the score in the target-rich environment. Most players looked at this strategy as cheating, but not the two boys in front of the line, the same two boys who'd attacked Leon at basketball.

Taylor studied his vest as he put it on. Being third in the long line, he hoped he'd recognize someone from school or church, but no one looked familiar. His father sat in a cushy chair in the waiting area, along with lots of other parents. He waved to his son when their eyes met.

Taylor's attempt to be friendly with the boys in front went unnoticed. They were having an involved discussion about another boy in line; he didn't know which one. They had begun whispering and making furtive glances toward someone down the line. Something gave Taylor the chills. He wasn't sure if it was the thunder in the background or something about these boys that didn't seem quite right.

Leon and Mendy stood in the middle of the pack, hoping in vain that the scumbags at the front hadn't noticed them. He told Mendy he was really glad she had come, acknowledging she'd made a great effort to be there. She shrugged and smiled at him. "Don't expect that you'll score more points than me. I think I'm going to be good at this game." She giggled, a sound he'd never heard from her before.

At 7:00 p.m. sharp, the check-in lady announced on the mic that there were three very special people in the group tonight. "Come forward if you turned thirteen today!" Surprised and reluctant, all three walked up front and stood next to each other as a rowdy version of "Happy Birthday" was sung. "Give it up for Taylor, Katie, and Leon!" the announcer hyped. Katie initiated the high five between the three, before each returned to their place in line.

"Let the onslaught begin!" the announcer roared as the players flowed into the darkened arena with their laser guns fully charged, ready for action. "Gonna Die Young" by Kesha was blaring as eyes struggled to adjust to the dark.

The lead boys, with experience and lack of scruples, set up fast and began scoring points, or "kills," before the eyes of their adversaries had adjusted to the darkness. Players were scattering, setting up behind mazes of four-foot walls, ready to defend themselves and inflict their own mayhem. Katie and Luke stuck together, hearts beating fast as they crouched behind a wall, taking aim at unknown assailants. Taylor chose to run from wall to wall, holding his arm over his vest to defray as many incoming shots as possible, all the while getting off shot after shot. Soon, even the novices understood the ping of "kills" and watched the electronic scoreboard record their increasing bounty.

Leon and Mendy hunkered down behind a distant wall, counted to three, and rushed out, taking several players by surprise. *Ping, ping, ping.* The strategy was working, and their numbers were moving up fast. Adrenaline was pumping.

As they crouched, ready for their next move, thunder clapped, averting their attention. Leon and Mendy didn't see the two players sneak up behind them, illuminated vests removed. The blow to the back of Leon's skull was swift and incapacitating. He lurched forward, hitting the ground before Mendy realized what had happened.

She saw them run and disappear into the maze. There were two of them, she was certain. She screamed for help, but the thunder and the sounds within the arena drowned out her cries. Two more people turned the corner, guns ready for points, and realized something wasn't right. A player was on the floor, with another waving her arms, shouting, "Help!"

Luke ran back to the front entry door, pushing people aside as he rushed to get help. Katie knelt with Mendy, not knowing what to do, but putting her arm around her as she yelled over the noise, "Luke is getting someone." Others came around the corner, including Taylor. He'd been schooled in first aid by his dad in a firefighter cadet program, where he learned how to slow bleeding down. He jumped into action. Throwing his vest aside, he pulled off his absorbent flannel jacket and held it tightly against the back of Leon's head, elevating it. Lights began to turn on in the arena, and they heard concerned voices. Luke was bringing help. Emergency services had been alerted, with a medic ambulance on the way, and probably police, too.

As parents flowed into the room, each praying it wasn't their child, the sounds of sirens could be heard. Michael, heart pounding, turned the corner of the last wall and saw his son—not unconscious on the floor, but instead rendering help to the injured young man.

Relief and fear gripped him. Thank heaven it wasn't his son—but would Taylor be accused of causing this, just as he'd been falsely accused so many years before?

Tony and Maria arrived seconds later. They knew it wasn't Katie, or any of their party guests, but they needed to find her, to see she was okay. John next, followed by Grandma, knelt by Leon, anguish on their faces. They nodded at Taylor as Mendy filled them in on what happened. She was sure who had done this, and when Taylor heard her story, he was able to add what he overheard the boys saying while he stood in line behind them. Now he understood whom the boys were talking about.

Paramedics arrived. They took over from Taylor, both patting him on the back for his quick action and thoroughly impressed when they learned he was only thirteen. "My dad is Tom Arthur," he said. "He used to be the fire chief." As they were lifting Leon onto the gurney, one of the first responders stopped a moment and smiled at Taylor, saying, "Good work." Michael was silent as he watched, feeling pride in his son and gratitude for Tom and Jenny—and more than a bit of sadness for all the time he'd missed with Taylor.

Grandma and Mendy followed the medic ambulance with John to North Bay Hospital. The police were taking Mendy's statement when the doctor walked over to say they could see Leon now. He was awake and doing well.

SIX

Katie crouched on her knees in her grandmother's garden behind their home. It was an organic garden, lush and brimming with an oncoming harvest of cucumbers, tomatoes, peppers.

Pulling weeds was not such a bad job, and it was one Katie had volunteered for this spring. Watching her grandmother grimace in pain as she had stooped to plant her garden in the last few weeks, Katie knew weeding was too much for her. Stubborn as ever, Bella insisted she could still take care of her garden. So every couple of days, Katie slipped outside to pull weeds while Bella napped. Her grandmother was the only person in her circle with whom Katie could never seem to win an argument.

Tony and Maria worked long hours at Bella's, and they had expanded their square footage to include space for an additional fifteen tables. They had to accommodate the ever-increasing clientele.

Katie always went to the restaurant to help. It was important. But soon after she entered high school, she made a masterful plea to allow study time after school, rather than go straight to the restaurant. She won that argument.

And her parents' reluctant agreement was rewarded when, soon after, Katie placed her report card on her mother's pillow.

Following a long, tiring day, Maria was about to turn off the light on the way to bed, when Tony noticed the paper sitting there. She picked it up, absorbed what it said, and whispered, "Tony, look at this. It's Katie's report card . . . and *every* single grade is an A—except one. It's an A+."

Grades in hand, they walked down the short hallway and opened her bedroom door, to find her sleeping peacefully. An open book lay beside her.

Maria closed the book with a bookmark and kissed Katie on the forehead, as Tony turned off her reading light, shaking his head in amazement.

At sixteen, a senior, Katie lugged heavy textbooks home after school most days and spent the first few hours on calculus and physics. English and history followed. She often found them a welcome reprieve.

One day each week after school, usually Wednesday, Katie volunteered at the Police Activity League Youth Center. It catered mostly to high school students from disadvantaged circumstances. She'd found a calling there of sorts, tutoring students. In addition to the PAL study room, where she spent most of her time, the facility had a full gymnasium, a boxing area, a "chill out" room with a big screen TV, and a well-appointed commercial kitchen.

On average, a hundred hungry teenagers walked through the PAL entry doors after school, seeking a safe place, friends, and something fun to do. Daily fresh fruit and healthy snacks, compliments of a giving community, along with monthly Rotary dinners, helped bridge the hunger gap for many of the students. Sheila, a retired middle school teacher with a talent in photography, ran the PAL and had become another mentor to Katie.

Katie first met Sheila at the public unveiling ceremony held at City

Hall, to which students from her leadership class at Armijo High were invited. Several of Sheila's framed and signed photographs, all with a local flavor, had been hung in the room named the Rotunda, just outside city council chambers. Katie had perused all eight pieces of Sheila's impressive work and found two favorites: one of a toddler's glee upon tasting his very first Jelly Belly and a veteran police officer's abject look of despair upon seeing yet another teenager shot to death due to gang violence.

The much-loved and admired mayor of Fairfield, Harry Price, was known by many as a consummate "community matchmaker." At events like this one, he tried to meet everyone and connect each person with someone they didn't know yet.

And this was how Katie came to volunteer at PAL. Mr. Price introduced her to Sheila, and they hit it off immediately. Katie went there as often as she could, to help kids study for tests and to keep them company. She did whatever should could, any chance she got, to help other people.

⁓

Monday morning, the bell rang precisely and reliably at 7:45 a.m., interrupting hundreds of fretful conversations around Armijo's campus. Another shooting had occurred over the weekend, not on campus but in front of a nearby apartment complex. Two young men were shot multiple times in a drive-by.

There was collateral damage. The random but lethal spray of gunshots caught a six-year-old girl while she was watching TV in her apartment.

Facebook spread the names of the young men who were fighting for their lives, and both were airlifted to separate trauma centers. Tragically, the young child had already succumbed to her injuries.

Like clockwork, a GoFundMe account had been set up to help pay her final expenses.

When she heard the news of this, Katie sat quietly in her chair, almost paralyzed. She forced herself to breathe. Anthony Simon was one of the PAL students she tutored every week. He was kind and smart. He had dreams.

Now his life hung in the balance—and for what?

How could this happen to him? Why did this happen? Full of questions and brewing anger, she barely noticed her teacher was speaking to the class, explaining that grief counselors would be available for students that day.

Katie thought about the grandfather she'd never met because his life had been cut short by a bullet.

She had to get out of there. She asked to go home.

Her teacher took a look at her, patted her on the back, and said, "Of course. Sam," she addressed the class TA, "please make sure Katie gets to the office okay. She's not feeling well."

Half an hour later, Maria picked up her pale, distraught daughter outside the school.

On the short drive home, Katie poured her heart out. She told her mother she knew one of the victims. "I've been tutoring him for months," she said. "And that little girl who died was doing nothing, just sitting on a couch watching TV . . . I don't understand."

Maria touched her daughter's cheek. "I'm sorry. I wish I had answers for you. My precious Katie."

At home, she hugged her daughter, and Bella hugged them both as their tears flowed.

Early the next morning, Katie heard through Facebook that both young men who'd been shot were doing better. Their prognosis looked positive. Maybe her prayers and those of most of Fairfield's would be answered.

She decided to stay in bed and not go to school. As she was never a child who had to be pushed to make the right decisions, Tony raised his eyebrow. He felt her forehead for a fever. There was none.

"Are you okay?" he said with as much sympathy as he could muster.

"I'm going to be all right, Dad. Like you say, I just have to work through a knothole."

They both smiled and he left for the restaurant with Maria. Bella would be keeping a close eye on her gifted granddaughter.

Katie sat in bed, her eyes open. Two hours passed. Bella peeked in again. It seemed like her granddaughter was in a trance. Bella was about to call Maria, when she heard some movement in Katie's room.

Helped by her walker, Bella went back down the hall to Katie's room. Still in her favorite Hello Kitty flannel pajamas, cheeks stained by yesterday's mascara, Katie was sitting at her desk, consumed with something on her computer. She glanced back at the open door and put her grandma at ease by giving her a silent "thumbs up" sign. Bella softly chuckled, relieved, then returned her arthritic version of the same sign. They both chuckled this time.

With the tip money Katie had earned working Friday and Saturday evenings at Bella's, she had bought herself her dream computer, an Apple MacBook Pro. It was the same one her friend and mentor, attorney Betty Lam, used. Although she missed her weekly trips to the library, the speed at which she could do her research astounded her.

Eagerly, she emailed her debate team teacher. "Is there still an open spot available for the NorCal High Schools Debate Tournament?"

Social studies teacher and debate coach Chuck Wood perked up when he read the email. He needed three students to enter the tournament and had only secured two. Katie would be his third, and with the strength she added to the team, he thought they might just bring home the trophy this year.

He checked the deadline to enter. It was today, which would give them four weeks to prepare.

The resolution for debate had already been set: "America is ready for sound and sensible gun control." After what had happened near their school the last weekend, Chuck felt certain he could finagle the affirmative side for his team.

He knew either side could win, depending on the debate skills and preparation. But his team would have a deeply personal interest in the affirmative side.

The first meeting of the team was set for Thursday after school. Katie texted Betty and asked for her help. She'd remembered seeing a handsome plaque on Betty's office wall, next to a Rotary plaque. It read, "University of California Berkeley Debate Champion." Betty was only too happy to help.

On Thursday after school, Katie walked into Mr. Wood's empty classroom. Desks were strewn in all directions. She wondered how many seconds it took a schoolroom to empty once the final bell rang. Falling or lagging in the doorway would be treacherous, she thought. Hearing the news earlier in the day from the principal that her friend Anthony and the other young man were continuing to improve had helped her feel upbeat. Still the only one in the room, she pushed several desks together in a circle, awaiting the others.

Voices echoed off the hall walls as Mr. Wood and Betty entered. She'd had to sign in before entering the locked campus, and Mr. Wood was called to escort her through the labyrinth of buildings.

The second member of the newly formed debate team, Cortney Harris, strolled in next, another no-nonsense student. Her jeans and top pressed as always, she wore perfect light makeup. She had a way of looking sharp even at the end of a long day. And, most importantly, she never lost an argument.

The third member, Luke Nobili, jogged in. The girls didn't seem to mind that he was still in his soccer uniform, wiping sweat from his forehead. He'd gotten permission from his reluctant coach to leave practice early for the meeting. Luke was competitive, willing to do the work to win—and he still harbored a secret crush on Katie.

All accounted for, Mr. Wood greeted the group. "Welcome to our first of many prep meetings in our quest to win back the NorCal Debate trophy. With the three of you and the addition of another seasoned coach, Betty Lam, we have a good chance. Thank you, Betty, for agreeing to help. What you may be happy to know is Betty was Debate Team Captain at Cal Berkeley!"

Cortney, with her innate ability to sense other's feelings, reminded everyone that their *coach*, Mr. Wood, had also earned a prestigious debate award from UC Davis.

With a wry smile, he moved forward. "Let's get this party started." He handed out the tournament format. "The resolution is set. We have the affirmative side. Now, do you want the good news first, or the better news?"

He had the circle's attention.

"Better news first!" Luke answered.

"Well, our five judges this year include State Assemblyman Jim

Frazier and State Senator Bill Dodd. So we should get some press."

Katie looked to Betty to gauge her expression. Betty's eyebrows were raised, and she nodded. Katie could see she was clearly impressed, and the wheels were turning.

Many years before, when Betty helped her dad, Katie had learned to trust her. With Betty as her Rotary mentor the last few years, that trust had grown into a friendship. So if Betty was impressed with who the judges were, then Katie was too.

"What's the good news?" Cortney asked.

Mr. Wood said, "David Lee High is our opponent."

The circle was quiet. When it had sunk in, Luke quipped, "And *that* is good news? They've won the tournament four times in a row. They were state champs last year."

With all the confidence he could summon, Mr. Wood slowly and deliberately looked each person in the eye, one by one, and then replied simply, "But they don't have all of *you*."

Cortney added, "Make that all of *us*, Mr. Wood, and I'm *in*."

———

The format of the debate they read outlined the precise sequences. The first speaker on the affirmative would start with ten minutes for arguments, followed by the same from the opposing side. The second speaker from each side would receive ten minutes for further arguments, identifying areas of conflict, and addressing questions from the other side. Five minutes would be allowed for each team to huddle and form their rebuttals, with the third speakers closing in five minutes. The opposing side would speak last. The five judges would then score each side and select the winning team.

Out of sixteen schools that signed up, there would be eight debates on different topics, on different days. Armijo and David Lee High were scheduled to close out the tournament. Based on skill sets, Mr. Wood suggested that Luke be the first speaker, Cortney the second, and Katie the final speaker. They all agreed. Prep meetings were scheduled for Monday, Wednesday, and Thursday at 3:00 p.m. Betty told the team she'd make as many meetings as possible and would be available after work for help with arguments, presentation, or research.

Each person's assignment for Monday was current research on the subject, focusing on the sensible gun control side for now. The opposing side's research, Mr. Wood said, they'd save for a couple of weeks. "One, two, three . . . let's do this!"

Three weeks flew by. The team had solid arguments in place, with visuals to emphasize their points. "One more time, Luke. This time look at your audience. Make them *feel* what you are saying—not just stating numbers and stats, but what they mean in lost lives. It's good to pause after a major argument."

Slightly annoyed, but with a desire to impress his audience of four for the fifth time, Luke rehearsed his opening. This time the result was a standing ovation from an audience that was hard to impress.

Cortney popped up next, anxious to show her prowess. Standing in front of her full-length mirror at home, practicing her part day after day, she came prepared.

The A+ she had earned in speech class was no fluke. She did well, practicing for expected opposing points. She felt good when she took her seat again. She knew there would be a few surprises from the opposing side, and she planned to buckle down that week to eliminate as many as possible.

As Katie slowly, thoughtfully, stepped up for her turn, the team was ready for the coup de grace. She hadn't missed a debate meeting. She brought mountains of research to the team and contributed enthusiasm and optimism.

But standing in front of the team, that day, it was different. She froze. She could not utter a word.

Eventually, she sank back into her chair. The group looked around at each other, stunned.

Betty knelt by Katie and asked, "What's wrong, honey? You've got this. I think you know this better than most people on the planet. Tell me what's happening."

No tears, just a sincere answer from a confounded Katie. "This feels personal. What I want to do is shout at the other side. Shake my fist at them! How can they be so uncaring, so devoid of compassion? I'm not sure I can do this . . . I'm sorry."

Betty, still kneeling by Katie, looked into her eyes. "And, my dear one, that is exactly why you need to do this. It feels personal because it *is* personal, and *personal* is different. Who better to make your position known in such a public way? You have the talent and passion. And, Katie," Betty paused for effect, "harness that passion, that anger, and you'll be able to create positive change. People are depending on you. I don't mean just those in this room."

The week leading to the debate that Friday afternoon was rushed. Despite the extra time allocated for debate prep, Katie didn't miss waitressing at Bella's on her obligatory Saturday evening, nor her Wednesday PAL tutoring session. She had a new PAL member who had signed up for her help with history, in addition to the other ten students she worked with weekly on various subjects.

Tall and lanky, with reddish hair, his name was Leon. And he seemed oddly familiar.

It was her goal to start each session by learning something new about her student. Leon smiled and asked if she remembered him. She stared at him, trying to remember where she'd seen him

"Oh, wait, Leon. Are you the boy at Scandia? Laser tag?"

"Yes," he responded. "I'm the one those idiots attacked. It's a good thing I have a hard head, or so my grandma says. And isn't your birthday January 2, 1999?"

Katie nodded.

"Mine, too. Do you remember, before we went in to play laser tag that night, they sang 'Happy Birthday' to three of us? Taylor, right down the hall in the boxing ring now, was the third one. He's the one who probably saved my life that night."

Katie sat speechless. She was recalling that night with clarity, her friends all cheering for her as she blew out thirteen candles, the stormy weather, and the shocking laser tag.

"Weird that we'd all wind up in the same place again."

Leon shrugged. "This isn't a big town."

Glancing at her phone, Katie realized she only had a few minutes until her next student arrived. Returning to the moment at hand, she asked if he'd like to come back in an hour, after her last tutoring session, so she could help him with history.

"Sure, and I'll bring Taylor for you to meet," he said.

More than three years had passed, but Katie recognized Taylor. They had clearly grown a lot, and she guessed both Leon and Taylor were over six feet tall. Leon was on the thin side, Taylor muscular.

Katie said, "So, you both like boxing?"

"Yeah," said Taylor, "I'm coaching him to be the tallest ever featherweight champion. He's coaching me to shoot 'threes' on the hardwood. Both goals may be impossible."

They all laughed as Leon and Taylor nodded at each other.

"So, do you still want history tutoring, Leon?" Katie asked, getting the distinct feeling tutoring was secondary.

"Nah, it's okay. I'll just read my book tonight. The test shouldn't be too hard."

Katie zipped up her backpack and put on her jacket as she readied to leave. She had a debate coming up on Friday, she explained. She had to practice for it.

<hr>

Mr. Wood had taken Friday off from school on his own dime to make sure the carefully prepared graphics were ready and working. Fairfield City Council Chambers, with excellent acoustics and a capacity of two hundred, had been selected for the DLH-Armijo showdown.

As he surveyed the cavernous room, Luke peeked in the doors and joined him. There were two tables with three chairs, each facing the front, where the combatants would sit. The judges' chairs were elevated, where city council members usually sat to make the tough decisions needed to run a community.

Mr. Wood and Luke were a bit awestruck at first as they looked around, imagining what would happen there in a few short hours. They were there to make sure the technology worked.

All was ready as the DLH coach and her coaching entourage entered. They shook hands and shared info on technology requirements and the layout of the room. She exuded the confidence of a coach who had many wins under her belt and was certain to add one more that day.

As the parking lot filled, supporters of both teams streamed into the council chambers. Local newspaper reporters from each city stood quietly in the back of the room. Trying to find seats together had become impossible, as the few seats remaining were singles. Sheila Webster was already snapping photos. As was standard procedure in every large public gathering, sharp-eyed uniformed police officers were on duty.

Each team was nervously doing last-minute prep in small, separate side rooms. The DLH coach tapped her metal pen on the table, gaining the attention of the packed room. Everyone went silent as all eyes focused on her.

"We're ready. We've done our research, practiced our arguments, and developed a strong and persuasive strategy." And then she paused, as if struggling with what to say. "In debate, we train to win, regardless of our personal beliefs. Does it really matter if you believe your side, so long as you convince the audience of your premise? It's about the prize, right? You are the leaders of tomorrow. Now go make me proud!"

At the same time, Mr. Wood and his team were huddled together, having made certain one more time that their cue cards were in order. All was ready. Betty noted how proud she was of each of them, and said that most of her Rotary Club would be in the audience, pulling for them. Mr. Wood nodded.

"I am proud of each of you," he said, "and your efforts to prepare, your commitment to the team. You are all outstanding orators with a powerful message, and most importantly, you *believe* in what you say. And what you say *matters*, because it's reinforced by that conviction. I'm proud to be your coach. You've got this. Now let's do it!"

The three Davis students walked out to the chamber and took their seats amid cheers from the crowd. All were seniors bound for prestigious universities.

Susan Chad would be first up for DLH, then Mary McCann, followed by last year's NorCal debate champ, Jeremy Cooper, wearing his brand-new cowboy hat and boots.

Heads held high, quaking inside but filled with resolve, Luke, Cortney, and Katie rounded the corner to see a packed room. Even the wide aisle in the very back had people standing four-deep. Among them were Taylor, Leon, and his grandma. Most were cheering. Grandma said she was reserving her applause pending the debate; after all, she did own a shooting range.

Family, friends, and community supporters were on their feet, most of them clapping—save one, who sat in the front row, crutches leaning on his aisle seat.

Katie recognized him. It was Anthony, her PAL friend who had been shot. She locked eyes with him for a moment.

He gave her a thumbs-up and a smile. She gave him a solemn nod.

Her nervousness melted away. Katie was on a mission.

Sitting in the middle of the five-judge panel up front was Fairfield's venerable mayor, Harry Price. With his warm smile, he stood, banging the gavel a couple of times to bring the room to silence. "We want to welcome our friends from Davis today for what we're calling Our Great Debate. And it's wonderful to welcome so many families, friends, and community members here to support Armijo High.

"I'm Mayor Harry Price, and I'm proud to introduce our panel of judges today. On my left is current President of Fairfield-Suisun Rotary Club Jerry Wilkerson and State Assemblyman Jim Frazier. On my right is State Senator Bill Dodd and Suisun City Manager Suzanne Bragdon."

Applause filled the room again. "Introducing our debate teams, and serving as the debate announcer, is Rotarian, author, and acclaimed speaker Dr. William Wesley."

Dr. Wesley went to the podium and explained the rules as the debaters' nerves peaked. He looked at the two tables of three speakers and asked if they had questions. All answered, "No, sir."

"Audience, please," he said, "no clapping or noise during the debate. Let's begin. Mr. Nobili, please take the podium."

Luke looked up at the judges, and with the crisp diction he'd practiced, he said, "America is ready for sound and sensible gun control." He then initiated his first proof source, which flashed to life on multiple screens around the room. "According to the U.S. Center for Disease Control and Prevention records, from 2005–2015, seventy-one Americans were killed from terrorist attacks on U.S. soil. During that same time, a staggering 301,797 were killed by gun violence.

"That is *three times* the population of Fairfield—every man, woman, and child gone due to gun violence. Of these, 58 percent were suicide, 38 percent homicide, and the rest accidental—including toddlers who found their parents' loaded guns.

"Data is unclear as to how many of these atrocities were caused by stolen firearms, but it is a substantial number. Question: Might we be ready for a reasonable law requiring gun owners to effectively lock up their guns? Would far fewer stolen guns and fewer deaths be a good thing?"

The next chart flashed on the screens. It showed stats from fifteen developed nations, among them Japan, Germany, the UK, Australia, Canada, and South Korea. Luke went on, "The murder rate in the U.S. from firearms is twenty-five times that of any other developed country per capita. Could that be due to the fact that we have more registered firearms than citizens, roughly 360 million? The ease with which people with bad intentions or with serious mental issues can obtain a gun in this country is shocking . . . and I mean legally, too, through glaring loopholes in current laws."

Luke looked at the judges and asked again, "Question: Is it time we close the loopholes so that it's actually difficult for domestic abusers, the mentally ill, and criminals to obtain lethal weapons?"

"Time," Dr. Wesley called.

Susan Chad, DLH's first speaker, stepped up and said, "America is not ready for more gun control. We don't need or want it."

Her first visual was the Second Amendment of the Bill of Rights. She carefully enunciated, "'A well-regulated militia being necessary to the security of a free state, the right of the people to keep and bear arms shall not be infringed.' And according to the Supreme Court's decision in 2008, their ruling that the Second Amendment protects the individual right to gun possession solidifies that. America is not ready for more gun control, because it is against the Constitution."

A colorful graph appeared on the screen, showing 57 percent of those surveyed on December 10, 2014, believed that owning a gun protects them from being victimized.

"And," Susan declared, pointing to her next graph, "a recent survey of Americans by Quinnipiac University clearly shows that a growing number of Americans support gun rights over gun control.

"It's very simple. According to public opinion, *and* the Constitution, there is no need nor any basis for more gun control than we already have."

She took her seat.

Dr. Wesley invited Cortney Harris to address the judges next. She held her carefully constructed index cards as she walked to the podium.

"The founding fathers of our great country had wisdom beyond reproach. Logic demands that they could not possibly have envisioned what our world looks like today—nor, I believe, would they have approved of, let's say, child pornography. Or thirty-round magazines and semiautomatic weapons used to murder a room full of innocent six-year-olds by a mentally ill teenager."

The stunned silence in the room was only broken when Cortney continued.

"No reasonable person would think this is what our founding fathers wanted to protect when they painstakingly crafted the Second Amendment. Thankfully, in fact, Congress had the wisdom to pass laws against child pornography, and they were upheld by the Supreme Court in the 1990s. And we believe our country is ready for sensible gun control now, just as we were when the scourge of child pornography was banned for the good of America."

Katie wanted to jump up and clap for Cortney, who had masterfully rebutted the Davis team. Instead, as was required, she sat quietly. The room hummed with whispers that would have to suffice for applause.

But Katie couldn't help glancing again at her nemesis, Jeremy Cooper. His folding chair was pushed back from the table, repositioned squarely, intimidatingly, toward the speaker's podium. Katie watched him, more and more annoyed. Instead of anxiously reviewing his stack of index cards like the other students, he sat motionless, staring at his boots. She wondered if he was bored, in a different world, or if something altogether different was going on with him.

Whatever it is, she thought, *this boy is galling.*

The low hum of the audience subsided as Cortney resumed. "Our last speaker was correct," she said, "when she showed us the graph demonstrating that a growing number of Americans are against gun control." Katie looked over at the previous speaker, who sported a newfound smirk. "But that same analysis found that when the survey asked follow-up questions of the same people, the results were dramatically different."

Another chart popped up on the screen, this one showing two questions:

> Do you favor universal background checks to prevent stalkers, domestic abusers and individuals with mental illness from purchasing guns of any type, from any legal source?
>
> Do you favor a requirement that gun owners be responsible for safely storing their weapons to keep them from easily being stolen, misused by family members, or accidentally winding up in the hands of children?

With her laser pointer, Cortney highlighted an astounding response to question one—76 percent, including Republicans, Democrats, and Independents, favor universal background checks, including at gun shows and private party sales.

She then read from the chart: "Question two received an even higher acclamation: 85 percent support a law requiring gun owners to lock up their guns or face consequences!"

Cortney glanced at the Davis table. No smirks there now. Addressing the judges one last time, with perfect posture and composure, she said, "Now is the time. America is ready for sensible gun control." And she took her seat.

Temporarily lost in the moment, Dr. Wesley rose slowly, inviting a now-subdued debater, Mary McCann, to the podium. Her coach locked eyes with her as she came forward, trying to exude confidence.

Mary hadn't given up. She was ready.

She began, "The old saying 'If guns are outlawed, only outlaws will have guns' has merit to many of us here. Who among us would choose to be defenseless if they or their family were attacked? You'll see on this graph that the states with the largest increase in gun ownership also have the largest drop in violent crime.

"Even law enforcement, specifically the National Sheriff's Association, has stated that it doesn't support laws that deprive any citizen of the rights provided by the Second Amendment.

"And let's look at the practicality of removing guns from people's homes. If the number of firearms is over 300 million in America, how can we possibly determine who has to relinquish and who gets to keep their guns?

"Gun owners make society safer, providing an effective defense when needed, and dissuading countless criminals from attacks. We'll never know how many crimes are stopped due to the fear of retribution."

Before she sat down, another two graphs were displayed, hammering her points home.

Dr. Wesley stood. "We will now take the predetermined five-minute recess so our debate teams can do final preparation for their closing speakers to present rebuttals. Armijo will begin when we resume. The clock starts now."

The two teams huddled together, engaged with their coaches. Clashes on both teams were evident, with Jeremy leading his team's heated discussion.

The judges exchanged looks. Low whispers sounded in the audience.

"Time," Dr. Wesley called.

Katie took a deep breath. She looked into the audience and saw her parents. Her mom was sitting next to Betty and their hands were clasped. Leon, his grandma, Taylor, several more of her PAL friends, including Ms. Heather who ran PAL, were wedged into the standing-room-only chamber. Katie stood and locked eyes for a moment with her friend Anthony. He nodded as his eyes projected strength and determination. She was ready. She had this, and Katie walked to the podium.

She began: "We feel firmly that America is ready for sensible gun control. Today both sides have presented research and data, much of it from bipartisan, respected sources. As you heard and saw, the data covers both sides, but with no clear message. This is personal to all of us, so let's do our own research. With the exception of our brave law enforcement folks, will everyone in the room who has personally used a firearm to defend themselves from attack please stand?"

The room was silent as heads turned in all directions to see who stood. Katie looked from side to side but didn't see anyone get up, so she added, "Will all stand who have a family member, close friend, or coworker who was saved due to carrying a firearm?" This time, one person stood, and a second person said that had probably happened to his brother. Katie thanked them as they sat down.

"Now, will everyone stand who has been personally affected or had a family member shot in gun violence?"

The room was aghast as Anthony, struggling with his crutches, rose.

Dr. William Wesley slowly stood.

Leon was already standing in the crowded back of the room. He raised his hand reluctantly, barely able to breathe as, once again, the trauma surrounding his sister returned to his mind's eye.

Solemnly, Grandma raised her hand too.

Taylor, with a sudden lump in his throat, thinking of the mom he never met, stood.

Cortney Harris, star debater, rose. Across the chamber, person after person awkwardly stood or raised a hand, each wishing they weren't among this mushrooming group.

Katie stepped forward and said, "I stand too. Thank you for your courage, and please remain standing. Now, will all who have had a friend, schoolmate, or work colleague killed by a firearm, please join us in standing?"

Nearly a third of the people in the room were standing, many of them moved to tears. The judges were riveted and appalled. Two of them were standing. In stunned silence, those standing lowered their hands and heads, and those with seats descended heavily back into the protection of a cushion and an armrest.

Then the unexpected happened. People jolted back into their moment of tragedy were comforted by strangers. A warm hug, a sympathetic pat on the back, an understanding look of solace permeated the room. It no longer felt like them-against-us.

Katie, shaking slightly, reached for her index cards. She tossed two aside, quickly glanced at the third, and began again as she nodded to Luke, who was ready with her next three visuals. "We are not advocating *no* guns, only three sensible laws which have been proven to save lives:

- Universal Background Checks with no loopholes, backed up with a strong Red Flag Law

- Gun Storage Requirement

- Ban Assault Weapons, including all versions of bump stocks and large capacity ammunition

The visuals featured on these slides were graphic: the first showed the faces of twenty people, various ages, who had been shot by people who should not have possessed guns; the second showed photos of children as young as two who had been shot as a result of a loaded gun being left accessible; the third was a photo of the child who had been shot in Fairfield a few weeks earlier, surrounded by more children murdered by someone with an assault weapon at Sandy Hook.

Looking at the audience, her voice raised slightly but still controlled, Katie declared, "It's *personal* to us. *We* are ready for sensible gun control. America is ready for sensible gun control. Now the only question is," and she turned back toward the judges, "do the leaders in our country have the *courage* to pass these laws?"

As she collapsed into her seat, there was pandemonium. Even the judges, unsure what to do at first, stood and clapped.

She glanced at the opposition table, where there were whispers and a dazed look on both of their previous speakers' faces.

Jeremy was not looking at his boots anymore. He seemed laser-focused, but she couldn't read his face.

Glad he was only the mediator of this debate and not a judge, Dr. Wesley turned his mic up.

Almost as an afterthought, Mayor Price, now seated again, pounded the gavel.

There was one more speaker to be heard, debate champ and cowboy from DLH, Jeremy Cooper. The audience, realizing there was another speaker, quieted, many feeling sympathy for anyone who had to follow Katie.

"Our last debater today is Jeremy Cooper. Please take the podium." Dr. Wesley felt a tinge of guilt, as though he were leading a lamb to slaughter.

Jeremy looked at his coach one last time before standing. She patted him on the shoulder, unable to look him directly in the eyes, and said, "I'll be proud of you whatever direction you take up there. You do what you think is right."

Jeremy hesitated. He slowly rose, pushing his index cards to the side, and left them on the table. As he stepped toward the podium, his boots felt as though they had lead in them. *Is this what guilty men feel heading to the gallows?* he wondered.

Gripping both sides of the podium, he said, "I represent the opposition to gun control. You may be happy to know I'm not going to show more charts and graphs. Instead, if it's all right with you, I'm going to speak from the heart.

"I grew up around guns. My dad taught me to respect their power, how to use them safely to hunt birds and deer, and on special occasions he'd even take me elk hunting with him. I learned to shoot skeet, and if I say so myself, I'm pretty good at it."

Several in the audience nodded, softly chuckling.

Jeremy continued in his calm, methodical drawl. "My best memories with my dad revolve around those times we had together, out in nature, flushing quail, bringing our limit back for dinner. He taught me so many things, but most importantly, he always told me to do what is right.

"Perhaps, like many of you, at eighteen I'm beginning to see how complicated that is—doing what's right. It seems there are two or more sides to almost everything, positions held by smart, passionate, good people. So how do we know what's 'right' when it comes to gun control?"

Katie was watching him intently. She now understood why he was the state debate champ. He was good, really good, and she wondered where he was going with all of this. She wanted to feel contempt for him, but she couldn't. He seemed like a decent guy.

He looked up at the audience as though he was speaking individually with each and every one. "Maybe we just need to care about our neighbors a little more, do a much better job of protecting our children—and yes, I believe that guns must be treated as the dangerous weapons they are. They are to be handled with care. To have guns is a privilege *as well as* a right.

"Mandatory universal background checks may make sense to you. The same with gun storage requirements, and even banning assault weapons. But there is no proof that these measures would keep us as safe as we want to be.

"There is no way for us to be as safe as we want to be. There will always be potential for harm. There will always be people who wish to do us harm. Wouldn't it be better to have a gun to protect ourselves?

"That's why we have the Second Amendment. It's a guarantee to every citizen in this country that, when the state fails to protect us, when the wolves are at the door and the police are miles away, we are permitted to have the means for keeping ourselves safe. For keeping our *children* safe.

"I realize how many of us have lost someone to gun violence. I've lost someone myself. I don't like saying it. I really don't. But the solutions the opposing team proposes are—"

He stopped midsentence. His eyes locked with those of Anthony, who sat beside his crutches, blinking up at the expert debater.

Jeremy coughed. He had been looking at the crowd the way he'd been trained to, roving across the crowd with his eyes so that his listeners would feel engaged. So they'd feel he was really talking to them.

But he hadn't really *seen* them. Now he did. And the display that Katie had instigated, of victims and friends and relatives of victims of gun violence making themselves seen, had transformed this crowd in his eyes.

He wasn't prepared for that. He cleared his throat.

He took a drink of water and looked down at his hands.

He seemed to whisper something to himself. To Katie, it looked like he was praying.

"Maybe you're right," he said, refocusing. "Maybe your solutions are the right solutions."

Jeremy seemed to lose himself for another moment. Katie and Cortney traded a glance.

"I just don't know," he said, straightening again. "I really don't. Can I say that? I'm not supposed to. I'm supposed to take my position and hold firm, no matter what. It's what I'm here to do. But I don't know if I can do that, given what's been said. This isn't just some competition. This is bigger than that. Isn't it?"

He looked at the audience as if he really wanted an answer.

"It's human lives we're talking about," he said. "People are dying." His voice broke.

Dr. Wesley raised his hand. "That's time, son," he said. "I have to cut you off there."

Jeremy swallowed hard and looked out at the audience. He looked pale.

He made his way back to his seat, boots pounding the floorboards. There was scattered clapping at first, and then a firm round of applause.

No one was certain what had gone through Jeremy's mind up there. But it appeared that something had spoken to him, something he needed to hear, and he had listened.

Katie saw Jeremy's coach reach over to where he sat and rub his shoulder. Jeremy looked at the floor and heaved a sigh.

For a moment, she thought she saw him smile to himself.

Tony, Maria, and Bella hosted a celebration dinner that evening. They hadn't stopped smiling since the end of the debate. They relived each moment with delight.

The back dining room at Bella's had filled up, and Katie sat at the center of the table. Her coach, Mr. Wood, brought his wife over to meet her. People took turns congratulating her.

Betty gave Katie a big hug, making sure she knew how proud she was of her, of all three debaters. Luke, Cortney, and their families were enjoying the adulation in the room too.

Even Mayor Harry Price showed up to the party. Finding the three debaters together, he expressed his pride in the job they did and added, "All of Fairfield should be proud of you. And by the way, did you know we filmed the debate? One of our staff said it was so good we should upload it to YouTube. What do you think?"

They were all for it.

By the end of the evening, they may have broken a record for hugs and laughter. It was an evening Katie would never forget.

That Saturday morning, Katie awoke with nothing to do. That was rare. She had nothing hanging over her that had to be accomplished. As the sun rose, she could see her cherished grandmother's garden taking shape. The grays began to take on a dark green hue, then lightened to a glistening neon. Katie breathed slowly, contented to watch the kaleidoscope of color emerge.

She hadn't yet seen what was occurring in the front of her home. Vans with letters on the sides, topped with oddly shaped antennas, were parked up and down her street.

The letters spelled out NBC, KUIC, CBS.

The debate had gone viral on YouTube. It had broken records. People had heard what Katie had said, and they wanted to hear more.

SEVEN

Taylor sat alone on the worn concrete bench, shivering in the holding cell, though he wasn't cold. March had brought unseasonably warm weather, even for California.

An hour earlier, his father, Michael, had given him the keys to his truck for a simple trip to pick up Saturday night pizza for them. This was a first; he never got to drive alone. Drake was on the radio, and Taylor's mind was on the scholarship interview coming up on Wednesday.

The traffic stop ahead was prompted by a 911 call that reported someone driving a blue Toyota pickup erratically.

"License and registration, please."

"Yes, sir."

Taylor fumbled for his license and handed it to the officer. Then he opened the glove compartment, hoping beyond hope he'd find the registration.

A Glock tumbled onto the seat instead.

The naïve eighteen-year-old, protected and nurtured by his parents, pleaded for the officer, now laser-focused, to believe him. The pistol wasn't his. He didn't even know there was a gun in the truck.

No spring chicken, the officer thought he'd heard that one a thousand times. They'd dust for prints, to confirm the kid's story.

As a solitary tear rolled down his face, Taylor thought of people who would be devastated to hear what had happened. His dad and mom, Ms. Heather at PAL, teachers, fellow explorers from his fire cadet program—all of them would be shocked.

But the biggest jolt was all his. No way could this be happening, he thought—this was not real. He thought, I've made good choices, I study hard and get good grades, I don't get into trouble . . . and I had no idea that gun was in my father's truck.

In the five years since Michael, his father, had come back, Taylor's life had settled into a comfortable rhythm as he moved back and forth between two worlds. He spent most weekends with Michael. For the last couple of years, they'd worked on restoring a boat that had sunk deep into the silt-laden delta. It had been hauled into Bert's Boat Repair, where Michael had worked since getting out of prison. The sixteen-foot wooden boat had so much damage, Bert declined the work, and the owner signed it over to him for disposal.

Something about that boat, though, drew Michael. Bert was happy to give it to him, as it saved him the cost of disposal. The rented house from the 1940s, where Michael lived and Taylor stayed most weekends, had a detached single-car garage where the future masterpiece fit perfectly.

The restoration would be a slow, methodical process. Michael patiently showed Taylor how to sand the mahogany planks at just the right angle and pressure. Taylor nodded, listening and watching intently, with a sudden pride in his father. Father and son spent countless tranquil hours together, lost in their own thoughts, wrestling their own demons. But both of them worked toward the same goal—maybe more than one.

—⁓—

Weekdays with his parents were different. Taylor arose early each morning for school. His father, Tom, liked to say, "The early bird gets the worm," and so Taylor tried not only to be on time but a few minutes early, like his dad.

"Hey, Taylor," said a schoolmate. "You ready for the chem test next period?"

Taylor shrugged. "Yeah, I'm ready."

"Well. Congratulations on the big award for good character. I heard you get a fifty-dollar bill. And you get to meet the mayor!"

Taylor shook his head and sighed. "I'm a little nervous about that. Being on a stage?"

"It'll get you ready to walk on the stage when you graduate," his friend said with a grin.

The principal had announced the winners of awards like Taylor's last week, on the intercom, after he explained the Rotary Good Character Award program. He'd shared that Rotary gives out twenty awards to local high school students, nominated by their schools for demonstrating exceptional good character: truthfulness, fairness, kindness, and helping others.

Each February, he'd said, Rotary held a ceremony to honor the winners and their families. He went on to say that students would walk across a stage to be congratulated by the Rotary president, the mayor, the superintendent of schools, and the fire and police chiefs.

At home that evening, when Taylor told his parents about the award, Tom cleared his throat.

He was trying not to tear up. He failed.

He hugged Taylor. Jenny wrapped her arms around them both,

remembering the frightened child who had knocked on their front door so many years before. And now he had grown into this accomplished young man with honor-roll grades. He had nice friends, and he was about to receive a Rotary award for good character. Of all the school events, teacher's conferences, Taylor's golf matches, and boxing tournaments they'd attended, nothing had made them prouder of him. She thought, as she looked at her son, that these were the traits that would matter, that would guide him to be a good husband, dad, and human being. Her heart was full.

Friday evening, at the KROC auditorium, Rotarians were busy preparing for the annual Good Character Awards ceremony. The *Daily Republic* writer had arrived, pen and pad in hand. She was conducting an interview close to the stage, close to where Taylor was sitting. He was near enough to hear what they said.

"So you are the current president, Mr. Wilkerson?" asked the reporter. "And why does Rotary put on this event every year?"

Good question, thought Taylor, still not quite believing he was getting an actual award.

Jerry Wilkerson, a recently retired banker, was thoughtful in his response, as always. "The reason we do this is to honor young people for making positive choices, sometimes in spite of formidable odds. Being truthful, fair, kind, and helpful to others—this is, in essence, being a good citizen. It not only bodes well for the student's future, but is also the foundation of a healthy community. The award is not designed for athletic prowess or academic scholarship. Students receive those awards elsewhere. *We* highlight students who model what Rotary represents in their everyday lives."

Taylor closed his eyes. He sighed. He couldn't believe this man was talking about him.

A camera flashed. Jerry began welcoming the first recipient and her beaming family. Student after student arrived, all with family and friends who were eager to applaud their children.

Tom and Jenny sat close to the stage. Cynthia Garcia, Taylor's social worker and forever friend of the family, sat in the seat Tom had saved for her. The handsome venue filled quickly as the lights dimmed and the speakers began. A lump rose in Taylor's throat.

Mr. Wilkerson welcomed the crowd. "Tonight we honor very special young people who are making our community a better place. Some have stood up to bullies in defense of another, some have tirelessly volunteered to help nonprofits feed the hungry or help others, and some have been inspirations for good at their high schools. So it is with great pleasure that we invite our award winners to the stage, to receive award certificates from Rotary and their community—oh yes, and that crisp, clean, fifty-dollar bill that is so popular! Please line up on the left side. And community leaders, please join me on the stage."

As the name of each recipient was called, they walked up the steps, hearts pounding, and shook hands with the mayor, district attorney, police chief, superintendent of schools, and fire chief, followed by Rotary President Jerry Wilkerson with the crisp fifty-dollar bills.

Taylor watched each recipient climb the stairs deliberately. One tripped but recovered easily, laughing at herself as she made her way to a firm, reassuring handshake.

Every time another award recipient stepped onstage, the audience's cheers were deafening. They resounded off the walls and grew and seemed to flood back to where Taylor was sitting, his hands shaking as he took it all in.

When he heard the announcer say, "Taylor Turner, please join us onstage," he stood on shaky legs and hurried to the stage. "Taylor," said the announcer, "was nominated by three of his teachers. One shared how he went out of his way to help special needs students, another how he brought resolution without violence as two students were about to fight. The last teacher told how Taylor had come to the aid of a student who had fallen off a twenty-foot stadium bench, breaking her leg."

Before Taylor knew it, he was on the stage, where he shook hands with the impressive group, one after another. The police chief looked him in the eye and told him, "Young man, I'm proud of you. If you have an interest in law enforcement, come see me."

Taylor stammered, "Thank you, sir," and continued down the line.

His head was spinning. The fire chief, who knew Taylor from the high school Explorer program, extended his hand next. He said, "Son, you were born to be a firefighter. Very proud of you."

Returning to his reserved seat, he saw Michael, waving at him from the back. Taylor already knew he was there—he'd recognized the joyous roar when he'd heard it. He smiled, knowing his mom would have at least two more scrapbook pages dedicated to this.

Tom was standing, still clapping, when Taylor reached his seat.

—◦◦◦—

Taylor felt like he'd been in the holding cell for hours. As he looked down at his hands, they still had fingerprinting residue on them. The realization of what was happening slowly washed over him.

He'd lose his scholarship chance. His goal of being a firefighter, like his dad, would disintegrate. He'd be barred from PAL, and he'd lose the friends he'd made there and in the Explorer program.

And then it hit Taylor: How would he face Tom and Jenny? Would they stop loving him? Was he being inexplicably drawn to prison, like a moth to a flame? Like Michael?

His hands wouldn't stop trembling. His whole body shook.

The cold metal screech of a key turning in the lock brought Taylor back to his somber reality. A sober-faced man entered, wearing a tan jacket with a tie that didn't quite match. He was flanked by the one man in the world he longed to see most—Tom, his dad.

Tom had been half-asleep in his easy chair, watching a rerun of *Chicago Fire*, when his phone rang.

"Hey, Tom, this is Joe. Joe Scholtes. I need you to meet me at the police station in thirty minutes. My officers have Taylor in a holding cell. He's all right, but he had a stolen gun in his glove compartment. Ballistics are being run now, and it looks like this may be the same gun used in the convenience store robbery last month, where two people were shot. Tom, I hate to have to make this call."

Sweat on his forehead, Tom tied his shoes, grabbed his jacket, and was out the door in five minutes, glad Jenny had already gone to bed. It would be better to let her sleep until he knew more.

Chief Joe Scholtes stood from behind his desk when Tom was escorted in. He wasn't there most Saturdays.

Not one to mince words, he said, "Damn, Tom, I'm glad you're here. I just gave this young man a Good Character Award a few weeks ago, at that Rotary event. Something just isn't right, here. We're running fingerprints on the gun. I hope like hell his prints aren't on it. He's already told the officer on the scene and our detective that he didn't know there was a gun in the vehicle. Taylor said the vehicle belongs to his father, Michael Turner. He's being brought in for questioning."

Tom sat where his friend motioned him to. He was glad to share an abbreviated history of Taylor and how he'd become Tom and Jenny's son.

"Joe," he said, "I know my son. He didn't have anything to do with this. He has been spending weekends with his biological father for the last few years. Michael seems like a pretty good guy, but he was in prison for years. Taylor was thirteen when Michael came back into his life. He's had a steady job for five years at a boat repair place. He seems to be on the straight and narrow. That's all I know for sure."

Both of them knew it would come down to evidence. But Tom was heartened to have Joe's support.

A detective led Tom through a maze of hallways with locked metal doors, and, Tom assumed, two-way mirrors, to Taylor's holding cell. He opened the heavy metal door. The moment Taylor realized it was Tom, a surge of hope returned.

It was fleeting. He stood, paralyzed, wanting to run to his dad, to have him make everything good again. Tom went to him instead, embracing his son. "I love you, Taylor. We'll get through this."

The detective said he'd give them a few minutes and left, closing the door behind him. As they sat quietly at the heavy metal table, Tom noted Taylor's every nuance, every expression. Without truly realizing it until now, his son had grown into a man—six feet tall, the athletic build of an adult, no longer the child he felt grateful to help raise.

Taylor was quiet, staring at the slick, gray floor. "Dad." He stopped. He could no longer look Tom in the eyes, this man he admired and trusted most in the world, the man who had taken him in when no one else would.

On the way to the station, Tom envisioned what his son would say to him and what the plan would be to exonerate him, how they'd come home and tell Jenny about it. It was just an unfortunate incident.

"Dad, it's my gun."

Tom was not prepared for this bombshell. He sat motionless, barely able to breathe.

"Son, what are you talking about? Why would you ever get a gun?"

Head hanging low, dreams crushed, broken, Taylor didn't answer. He couldn't look at his dad.

Just then, the detective stuck his head back into the room. "We have Michael Turner in custody down the hall. He says the gun isn't his. We'll soon find out. Taylor, is there anything more you want to tell us?"

Taylor was about to offer his confession for the gun, but Tom intervened. He placed a firm hand on Taylor's arm. Tom had to stop him. He knew his son was willing to throw away his entire future to protect his father.

"No, detective," he said. "Taylor knew nothing about that gun. No disrespect, detective, but I think it's time we got an attorney."

Detective Sortor nodded. He understood.

Matt Lucas dreamed he was sipping a piña colada poolside in Maui when an irritating ring awoke him. Fumbling for the phone, he knew from experience that at 2:30 in the morning it wasn't good news.

A familiar voice on the line said, "Matt, I'm sorry I had to wake you in the middle of the night. This is Tom, Tom Arthur, from Rotary. Taylor is in a world of trouble. We're at the police station."

"Tom, that's all you need to say. Fairfield PD?"

"Yes. In a holding cell."

"Don't answer any more questions. I'll be there shortly."

Tom, with a sigh of relief, said, "Thank you," but Matt had already pressed the red button.

PC Joe Scholtes watched as his most experienced fingerprint specialist worked her magic. She'd dusted the Glock, only to discover that it had been wiped clean of anything usable. Someone had been thorough.

But they didn't know her. Joan didn't give up easily, and knowing that the PC was personally invested in her findings, she was even more determined.

She had painstakingly removed the two bullets from the chamber. "Come to mama," she quipped absentmindedly, fixated on the prey.

Scholtes grinned for the first time that night. If anyone could find a print, it was Joan. And he was hoping they were anyone's but Taylor's.

—~~~—

Tom and Taylor sat silently next to each other, both of them grateful that Tom had been allowed to stay with him.

Neither of them knew what to say. Tom opened his mouth to speak, but closed it before any words escaped. Taylor sighed, over and over.

"Matt Lucas is on his way," Tom finally said.

Taylor kept looking forward, facing the wall, beside Tom.

"Do you remember him?" Tom said.

"We sold pumpkins," Taylor said. "At the Rotary fundraiser."

"That's right."

"I like him."

"Good. He's a top-flight attorney, Taylor. We're going to get this taken care of."

Taylor shut his eyes tight. "I'm so sorry," he said.

Tom put his arm around Taylor and pulled him tight.

"This is going to be okay, somehow," he said.

"Is this going to cost you money?" Taylor said, pulling back gently, rubbing his eyes. "I think I have like three thousand dollars in savings . . . for college."

Tom had his hand on Taylor's shoulder. "You aren't going to touch that money. Taylor, we'll make this work. What you need to do right now is let Matt talk to the police. Don't tell them anything; don't say anything."

Taylor put his hands over his face. "That makes me sound like a criminal," he said.

"That's not what it means. It means you're being smart. You're letting Matt do his job."

Taylor nodded. The fog of confusion was starting to lift. People who cared about him were there to help him.

Tom put his arm around Taylor. "Son, I need you tell me straight, right now: Did you have anything to do with that gun?"

"I don't want my father to go back to prison, Dad. It will kill him. I can't imagine he had a gun. He always tells me to stay away from them—that I'm safer without them. So, no. I didn't know the gun was there."

"Good," Tom said, sighing with relief. "I knew it. You're a good kid, Taylor. We have nothing at all to worry about."

Matt was escorted down the maze of holding cells and interrogation rooms he knew so well. He figured he'd probably been there more times than the youthful officer he was following. As the officer opened the door and Matt walked in, the seasoned criminal attorney felt his adrenaline kick in. This is why he'd opted for criminal defense law. The money and the hours weren't great, but seeing the look on people's faces when he opened that door kept him coming back. He needed to be needed.

Sporting yesterday's crumpled shirt, he pulled up a chair across from a wide-eyed Tom and a fidgeting Taylor. "Fill me in, guys. I heard a little bit from Detective Sortor in the waiting room. Taylor, tell me what happened from the beginning."

Taylor felt a thread of hope. "Michael said I could drive his truck to go pick up a pizza. I was on my way to Round Table. Then the cops stopped me."

"Stop," Matt said. "Don't leave out any details. Tell me everything that happened, step by step."

"Okay," Taylor said. He swallowed. "I was at a stop sign. I came to a complete stop. I always do at that intersection, because it's only a two-way stop, and people come flying down there."

Matt nodded. He wrote all of this down on a legal pad. He had a tape recorder going as well.

Taylor said, "I was turning right on Sunset Avenue when I saw the light from the police car. I pulled over right away. He came to my window. I rolled it down. I was nervous. I gave him my license, and then I opened my father's glove compartment to see if there was a registration in there. A gun fell out. I couldn't believe it. I just stared at it. I tried to tell the officer I didn't know anything about it, but I don't think he believed me. So, here I am. The detective said they brought my father in for questioning. They won't let me see him. I'm afraid he'll have to go back to prison. Mr. Lucas, please don't let that happen. "

Matt looked up from his legal pad and studied Taylor. Because he often sat next to Tom at Rotary, he knew quite a bit of the history behind these two, how Taylor had come into Tom and Jenny's life, how they'd grown into a true family.

And he understood how devastating this might be for all of them. "Okay," he said. "Tom, what can you tell me?"

"Matt, my son didn't know about that damn gun. He had nothing to do with it. I'll stake my life on it. He's a good kid, and how this thing happened, I don't know. When Chief Scholtes called me at home, around 10:00, I rushed right here. He told me the officer was dispatched after a 911 call came in. The caller reported erratic and dangerous driving, an old blue Toyota pickup matching the one Taylor was in.

"Apparently the officer told the chief that he didn't observe any driving issues himself. He said Taylor was cooperative. He said he was respectful to him! So when the gun fell out of the glove compartment, the officer said Taylor looked as shocked as he did." Tom stopped, trying to maintain his composure, then continued, "And Matt, there's something else. The same gun may have been involved in a robbery last month. Two people were shot."

The room went dead silent. Matt watched as an incredulous expression appeared on Taylor's face, his head shaking, his mouth agape.

Matt prided himself on being a good judge of the innocent and the spurious. Taylor was innocent; Matt could feel it. This sealed the deal for him. Finishing his notes, he returned his prized Mont Blanc pen to his shirt pocket and closed his portfolio. "Let me see what's happening with the fingerprints," he said. "I'm going to try and get you released, Taylor, so you and your dad can go home. Hang tight. I'll be back."

"Don't forget Michael," Taylor shot back.

Matt gave a weak response. He glanced at Tom. "I'll find out what I can. Taylor, you are my first concern."

———

"Jesus, Mary, and Joseph!" Joan exploded. She'd been foiled for hours, trying to get that one print, even a partial, from the gun or ammunition. At last, she had it. The partial came from the bottom of the second bullet—good enough, she hoped. The chief had gone home a few hours before, but left strict instructions to call him immediately, if she was able to determine whose print she found.

Joan sighed. As she began the match process, like so many times before, she couldn't help but reflect on what was riding on this. Lives would be impacted forever, for good or ill.

Sometimes she felt like the Grim Reaper—but not tonight. At least not for Taylor.

———

Matt returned to the interrogation room with the good news. The print on the bullet wasn't his.

Tom and Taylor wept and hugged. Matt stood quietly, contemplating this duo that looked unlike one another, but were perfectly matched. "No record of any kind will follow you, Taylor. Assuming nothing unexpected comes up, this will be a distant memory for you soon. Want more good news?"

They pivoted back to Matt, with full on attention. "The print didn't belong to Michael, either."

"So who put that gun in the Michael's glove compartment?" Tom said.

Matt simply responded, "They have some leads, and they're working on them."

But he knew more than he could legally tell them. Sortor had told him that Michael's truck, especially the passenger side door and glove compartment, were being dusted right then.

———

Tom pulled up in their driveway, a ten-minute drive from the station. Taylor's head had dropped forward. There was a soft, peaceful rhythm to his breathing. As Tom removed his keys from the ignition, he sat still, exhausted, watching his son sleep. He thought about his thirty-five years as a firefighter and how many times he'd seen one moment change a life forever.

A feeling of gratitude overwhelmed him. Gratitude that his precious son would be able to continue on his journey they'd all hoped and worked for. Gratitude for his friends who stood behind him and believed in his son. And gratitude that no lights in house were on yet—Jenny had slept through it all.

A couple of weeks later, Matt called Tom to see if he'd like to meet for lunch.

Village Café was busy, as usual, filled with people who smiled with recognition at Tom and Matt. As the waiter set their lunch on the table, Matt explained he'd heard rumors that the police had someone in custody for trying to set up Michael. A guy who had worked at Bert's Boat Repair, Jacob something, had sneaked the Glock into Michael's truck while he was at work. The prints on his passenger-side door proved it, backed up by the hidden camera Bert had installed after a vandalism issue a few months before.

The theory was that Jacob was involved in the robbery the month before and had decided to set up Michael, a convicted felon and an easy mark, so the police would throw the book at him. Jacob would be off the hook.

He didn't anticipate that Taylor would be at the wheel when he called 911 to report the hoax of an erratic driving claim.

So that was it, by all accounts. Case closed.

Tom reached across the table and shook Matt's hand. "I can't thank you enough," he said. "You saved my son, my family. I fully expect to pay for your time. So whatever your bill is, Jenny and I are ready."

"I appreciate your kind words, Tom. But other than getting up in the middle of the night, there wasn't much for me to do. Everything fell into place on its own. Something you could do for me, though? Save me a good seat at Taylor's graduation."

EIGHT

Leon, now sixteen, had grown into a tall, lanky kid, quick on the basketball court. The high school coach called him "Dead Eye" for his precision—he could sink a three-point shot under any sort of pressure. But to the chagrin of the varsity basketball coach, his passion wasn't basketball.

He'd spent the last ten years of his life, ever since his sister was killed, with his attentive dad and his adoring, slightly overprotective grandma. They had lived together at the family home near the Phillips Gun Range, the business she'd owned and run for forty years.

When she passed away the previous fall, as a fitting goodbye, twelve of her most faithful customers honored her with their version of a twenty-one-gun salute. One-eyed Bob Facebooked his buddies about the time and place. When the hard-core group pulled up in a variety of prized pickups with gun racks, several of them modified and noisy, they brought enough guns for a militia. Bob silenced the motley collection of characters as he bowed his head and said in a subdued tone, "Lord, open your arms to our sister, and if anyone gives you trouble up there, you can count on her to have your back." With that, twelve firearms poised, they opened up on the heavens with power rarely seen outside of battle. John and Leon knew Grandma would have liked it, as each of them wiped away a tear.

She was laid to rest under a giant oak tree in Rockville Cemetery, next to her husband. John thought, as the service ended, that now the two were together again. And, just like Grandma, everything had been planned and paid for far ahead of time. He guessed she had even planned the beautiful fall day . . . yep, that was his grandma.

Leon tried hard to be strong. Grandma—really his great-grandma—had been his guardian angel. After she and his dad rescued him from Nevada, she was the one who would hold him when the tears flowed and when they wouldn't flow but the hurt was overwhelming.

She was the one who insisted upon therapy for him. For two years, she drove him once a week to the therapist and sat with him as he wrestled the demons created by his trauma. Leon remembered Grandma wiping her own tears as she quietly listened to him and his therapist talk.

He never had the chance to share with her what that meant to him. And now she was gone. One more hole in his heart. Instead of feeling sadness, he slammed his fist into the trunk of the oak tree.

With a partial cast on his right hand, that night Leon sneaked into Grandma's gun range, where he found the keys to the safe where she kept the guns and ammo. Oblivious to the pain in his hand, he grabbed the weapon he'd always wanted to use, but which Grandma forbade—the AR-15. In the shooting area, with multiple clips at his side, an unused target hanging before him, he unloaded holy hell.

The target disintegrated, but Leon barely noticed. He was shooting at the ghosts who had haunted him since he was five years old.

Adrenaline spent, the calm he had unknowingly sought descended upon him. Leon had discovered a passion.

A few months later, John and Leon sat in armchairs around a mahogany conference table with fresh flowers as the centerpiece. Their longtime family attorney, Mr. Hillman, had called them to share his condolences and let them know Grandma had recently completed a trust.

As Mr. Hillman shared the trust's contents, John listened closely. Leon was absorbed in Clash of Clans on his cell, pretending to be interested in the conversation. But when he heard Grandma had given him her immaculate 1999 Ford Taurus, his ears perked up.

Grandma had always kept her finances private, and John barely understood her financial status. Mr. Hillman shared that the home would now be transferred to him. There was a small mortgage, and John thought he could afford it, due in part to the raise he'd recently gotten at work. The Phillips Gun Range was his as well, but Grandma had emphasized in the trust document that it would be best to shut it down, as it had operated in the red for the past year. A new, better-equipped gun range had opened across the valley.

That suited John fine, as he had no interest in running a business. He was happy with his job as head of maintenance at the swanky, exclusive resort in Napa Valley, The Grape Seed. With the promotions he'd earned over the six years he'd been there, he was able to provide the stable income that allowed him to raise Leon and was easier physically than pounding nails eight hours a day—especially since he'd put on forty pounds or so, most of it around his middle.

The last item mentioned in Grandma's trust was a surprise. She'd instructed Mr. Hillman to specifically reference an antique wooden cigar box with a red-haired boy's face on top. It was more sentimental in nature, she'd said. She didn't want her boys, John and Leon, to overlook its contents.

Driving down the two-lane country road on their way home from town, John stopped at the mailbox. Leon hopped out to pick up the normal barrage of bills, the monthly publication of the U.S. Firearms Association, which John always looked forward to, and advertisements. As he opened the mailbox, his body stiffened, and he froze for a moment. The return address of the letter on top said simply *Trina/ Mom*. It was addressed to him.

Over the nearly ten years Trina had been in prison at Chowchilla Women's Correctional Facility, she'd written many letters to Leon. Grandma or John, whoever retrieved the mail that given day, would read through it, shake their head in disbelief, and toss it.

Until now, the underlying theme was always the same: "Why me? Why doesn't anyone come to visit? It's miserable here." Not one letter had seemed remorseful or, they felt, indicated a sincere interest in how Leon was doing—so, for years, she wasn't even mentioned to him. It was easier and kinder, they'd decided, to simply say prison didn't allow Trina to send letters.

Eventually, the flow of unanswered letters slowed to a trickle. The last few years, an occasional letter would arrive. Grandma surmised that Trina was writing them as a form of therapy, for herself.

Leon sat back in the truck with his hand on the letter, staring out the window. His face had turned pale and his eyes distant, a slight tremor in his hands. The memories he'd tried to forget came crashing back: being beaten by Trina and then by Billy in some filthy bathroom. Worst of all, he saw Sara slumped in the backseat with terror in her eyes and their mother's screams. "Leon, what have you done, what have you done?"

When they stopped at the house, Leon's dad opened the passenger door and placed his hand on his shoulder, attempting to bring him back from the purgatory he alone knew.

Leon stood. His dad wrapped his arms around him. When they finally entered the house, Leon took the unopened letter and stuck it in his jacket pocket. Then, with an unexpected grin, Leon asked if they could go to the gun range.

John had carefully chained and padlocked the exterior doors to Grandma's pride and joy. Soon after Grandma passed, someone had entered the gun range and unleashed a couple hundred rounds of havoc, opening the fortified gun closet and damaging walls not meant for shooting. Oddly, nothing had been stolen, but the place was a mess.

He suspected Leon, but never asked him about it directly, and was instead careful to stop future access to the range by his son or anyone else who might try to break in. John was now confident the arsenal of firearms was safe behind multiple locks and keys. Opening up the gun range was a big ordeal. John did his best to talk Leon out of going, but Leon was determined, and after what had happened with the letter, John wasn't of the mind to turn him down. "Please, Dad, I really need to go," Leon said.

John thought his choice of the word *need* was odd. But he acquiesced. *Maybe it will be good for him*, he thought.

———

John unlocked the door to the gun range. As each barrier to entry was eliminated, Leon's heartbeat sped up. Cobwebs and dust had taken hold of the once-busy interior, and an unwelcoming, musty smell was in the air. John grabbed yet another key from his belt to unlock the gun and ammo closet.

Leon could hardly wait. Something about shooting a gun, the real deal, made his adrenaline kick in.

The door of the gun closet now open, Leon guessed there must be fifty guns, all shapes and sizes. There were pistols, some small-caliber, Glocks, several shotguns, rifles, semiautomatics, and even two long guns. John was struck by how mesmerized Leon was as he checked out the arsenal. Following his gaze, he realized Leon seemed to be looking for a specific weapon, and when he found it, on the back wall, recently cleaned, his eyes rested there. It was the AR-15 that had been used in the break-in.

John finally asked Leon if he was the one who shot up the gun range a few months back. But Leon didn't answer—not because he was trying to avoid owning up to the truth. He was simply in a trance, in a different place.

John was unsettled. On the third try, with a nudge from his dad, Leon came back to the present. He answered more in the form of a question, "Yes, it was me?" No elaboration or excuse—that was it.

"Dad," he implored, "can I use the AR-15?"

This time it was John who was speechless. At last he gave a reluctant "yes."

As they entered the indoor gun range, each with his weapon of choice, John's a .45 pistol and Leon's the AR-15, Leon carefully pulled the unopened letter from his jacket pocket and walked down to place it in the center of a new target. Returning, earplugs in place, guns poised, John nodded to his son to start.

A minute later, sweat dripped from Leon's face, the entire target annihilated. John stood wide-eyed with no shots fired from his .45. He knew for sure now who had broken into the gun range and wreaked havoc a few months before. And Leon's aim had clearly improved.

—⁓—

As his grades in school declined over the past few months, Leon had settled into a kind of regimen. After school, he'd drive the shiny '99 Ford Taurus home, wash and vacuum it, and fiddle with the engine if any sound seemed out of the ordinary. Then he'd jump into his newfound obsession, video games—*Head Shot* in particular. Since its recent introduction, *Head Shot* had become the most popular game for teenage boys on the market, providing mind-numbing violence through gun battles, including "taking out" random people to score extra points. He had three hours to spend as he pleased before his dad came home from work, and it flew by each day as his skill at earning extra points elevated.

John would often stop at Arby's or Taco Bell on his way home and grab dinner for them. Sitting across the table, they'd share the news of their day. Leon would mostly talk about his car, his plan to change the tires and rims, maybe even paint it later.

Even after a long day at work, John was animated when he talked about his day. Working at arguably the most exclusive resort in Napa Valley, celebrities were commonplace. His job was to maintain each unit's plumbing and electrical systems, erect gazebos for special events, and do whatever else might be necessary to help warrant the three-thousand-dollar-per-night average room rate. Per the resort rule, John never disclosed names of guests, even to Leon, but he would give hints. One week, an Emmy award-winning actress would be onsite with her three giant foo-foo Newfoundland dogs. The next week it might be an "in-the-closet" country singer heartthrob, a Fortune 500 CEO and his "assistant," and a media icon. Everyone staying at the resort was somebody. And most were friendly and generous with tips and compliments.

Leon loved hearing his dad's stories, especially because his dad lit up as he told them. John was proud of his job, and Leon was proud of his dad.

One Saturday John packed a picnic lunch of ham and cheese sandwiches, chips, and bottled root beer (Leon's favorite) for the two of them. Leon thought they were going to The Grape Seed, but instead John drove past it and proceeded a few minutes up the hills behind the resort. There, hidden by hundreds of old oaks, was a level place only a minute's walk from a rarely used, one-lane utility road. It was perfect for a picnic.

As they set up their weathered folding chairs with a view of the town of St. Helena in the background, they could see the lush, grassy area of the resort, with its perfectly manicured landscape. Well-dressed people were milling around a gazebo flanked by maybe fifty chairs, all adorned with burgundy ribbons. Urns with magnificent hot pink flowers dotted the scene. Tuxedo-clad musicians were setting up to play.

Leon couldn't contain his question any longer: "Dad, who's getting married?"

His dad conveyed by his expression that he couldn't say, but with a hint of a smile, he pulled a pair of binoculars out of his backpack.

Relaxing and enjoying the comradery of the special day, father and son relished their sandwiches and chips and gulped the still-cold root beer from the bottles. As the event before them began in earnest, the diverse guests were seated and the tempo of the music changed. Leon picked up the binoculars as a pretty browned-haired girl walked down the aisle between the chairs. He studied the seated guests. Several looked familiar, though he couldn't initially place from where. When the music momentarily stopped, all the guests rose to hear a Grammy Award-winning rendition of Mendelssohn's "Wedding March" and watch a beautiful bride walk the aisle alongside an older, dignified man—probably her dad, Leon guessed. She wore a flowing white sleeveless dress, accentuating her athletic figure and an armful of tats on her left arm. John watched Leon's expression as he focused the binoculars and at last recognized the bride, gymnast Shar Thurmond, whom America had fallen in love with during the last Olympics.

Leon and his dad talked all the way home about their day, both agreeing it was one of the best ever. They said they'd have to do it again. John smiled and felt content for the first time in a very long time. He could tell his son was proud of him.

———

The antique cigar box, described in Grandma's trust, had been an afterthought the last several days, with so much going on. John had even gone to the doctor after not feeling well, something he hated to do. The doctor told him his blood pressure was high and that he should lose weight. *No shit, Sherlock,* he thought to himself. He was given a prescription and told to come back for a follow-up appointment in a couple of weeks.

At school, Leon was having trouble too. A couple of older kids jumped him by the lockers, and with his six-foot, 140-pound frame, he was no match. They stole his backpack, warning the sophomore not to squeal.

He didn't tell anyone at school, but his dad was persistent in learning where he'd gotten the scrape on the side of his face and his sore shoulder.

Instead of heading straight to the school principal, like Leon feared, John told his son they would find a boxing program.

That night, they went to dinner at their favorite Mexican restaurant, Bella's. Both were hungry and began to relax as the chips, salsa, and drinks arrived at the table. Draft beer was still John's favorite; Leon settled for root beer. As they talked about the week, including the meeting at Mr. Hillman's office, they remembered the antique box. They vowed to look for it when they returned home that night.

Steaming enchiladas with melting cheese arrived, served by a pretty young girl named Katie. John couldn't help noticing that Leon sat up a little straighter and smiled when she was at the table. And John couldn't help but smile at Leon's reaction. Happy, with full stomachs, they drove home excited. They were on a quest to find Grandma's cigar box.

It felt strange, almost indecent, to rummage through Grandma's bedroom and closet. John had been avoiding cleaning it out. Doing so would feel so permanent, he knew. But looking for a treasure, at the direction of Grandma—now, that was something else.

It was fun. They attacked the hunt as a game, each picking specific areas to explore, not expecting much difficulty. They searched under the bed, in the nightstand, through the neatly ordered chest of drawers, high and low in her closet. Nothing. Then John entered her small bathroom, with room for one. Nothing.

They grinned at each other. This was just like Grandma. She was making them work for it. And then, at the same instant, both knew where it was.

They rushed down the hall to her sewing room. There, in the

bottom drawer of a plastic cabinet, next to her chair, was an ancient-looking box with a drawing of a red-haired boy on top, complete with protruding ears and a smile. They'd found it.

Setting it on the kitchen table, they carefully lifted the lid, unsure what awaited them. The box was full, and on the top was a one-page note. In Grandma's handwriting, it said, "My dearest John and Leon, you found the box! Contained here you will find many items of significance to me, and hopefully to you too. Know you are both loved. Be good to each other. Grandma. P.S.: Don't forget to feed the dog." Confused, they looked at each other and both broke out in hysterical laughter—they didn't have a dog. Even now, she had a way of lightening things up, just when they needed it most.

Next in the box were photos: John holding newborn Leon; Grandma holding him; Sara sitting on Grandma's lap next to John, who was holding Leon. And there were several of Sara and Leon playing together at the beach, probably at Tahoe.

Noticeably missing was any sign of Trina. There were three pictures of Grandpa, one looking down the barrel of a rifle, another looking proud in front of the Phillips Gun Range sign, and an old black-and-white of a young couple getting married.

A plastic baggie containing a gold cross and chain followed, with a sticky note attached that read: "This belonged to your grandpa. He told me it protected him from harm, and I hope it will you too." The note didn't specify who should wear it, but John handed it to Leon. "Maybe this will keep you safe from the hoodlums at school. This and boxing lessons," John said. They both smiled.

Beneath the baggie was a folded newspaper page. As Leon unfolded it, he noticed it was the front page of the local Daily Republic newspaper, dated of January 4, 1999. A penciled arrow, probably by Grandma, pointed at a picture of three babies, side by side in a hospital nursery. One baby was circled.

As Leon read the description below the picture, he was startled to see his name. His dad confirmed, "Yes, you were on the front page of the newspaper!" Leon carefully refolded the page and placed it in his wallet to read the lengthy article below the picture later.

Lastly, at the bottom of the cigar box was a sticky note atop a small stack of $100 bills and two three-day passes to Disneyland.

That final yellow sticky note said to have fun and ride Space Mountain once for Grandma.

The boxing program at the Fairfield PAL Teen Center had been a good fit for Leon. John especially liked the coach. He'd read about Mr. Padilla, who had not only been a successful fighter, but had spent the last twenty years helping local kids learn the sport and develop confidence and self-control. Three days per week, Leon drove his spotless Taurus to the PAL Teen Center after school. Leon's spindly physique had transformed since the last year with the help of a weightlifting regimen and a better diet, both part of Mr. Padilla's overall boxing program. He was now 6'1", like his dad, and 160 pounds of "pure muscle," according to his proud father.

Leon's eyes stung from the dripping sweat. He wiped his face with a towel. The punching bag was still standing after his workout finished, but his coach wondered how that was possible. He'd full-on attacked the bag today, punching relentlessly until he couldn't lift his arms.

Coach Padilla had watched knowingly as Leon's pent-up anger surged through his limbs into the worn leather. He'd seen it all before with troubled young men, hundreds of times. Kids came into his boxing program for exercise, to hit something or someone without consequences. Many of his athletes carried a life of heavy baggage through the doors, and most of them, he hoped, left with less of it. His gifts to those who came to him were a healthy way to cope with life and some tools to help them succeed. Leon was a formidable work-in-progress.

There was another reason why Leon kept coming to PAL. He'd made a few friends, chief among them Taylor and Katie.

The article that Grandma left him with his photo in the paper went unread for months, forgotten, neatly folded in his wallet. Sitting in a waiting room, while his Taurus was being smogged, his phone dead, he absentmindedly looked through his wallet.

There it was. As he carefully unfolded the yellowed newspaper article and began reading, he found it was not what he'd expected.

The mechanic yelled his name, to say his car was ready, but he didn't look up. There, along with the picture of three unrecognizable babies—Leon, Taylor, and Katie—was an article about a murder.

Taylor never talked about his birth mother, and now Leon understood why. It wasn't that she was a druggie, abusive and in prison like his own mother. Instead, she'd been an innocent, loving mom about to give birth to a son when she'd been mistakenly shot in a drive-by. The mechanic yelled his name again, to pick up the keys. But as he glanced over at Leon, perturbed by the delay, he saw tears flowing down his cheeks.

The mechanic left the keys on the counter and returned to the garage. He wondered what that was all about.

Later that week, at PAL, Leon showed the article to Katie.

"Katie, you're in this newspaper article," he said. "At least, you're in the picture with Taylor and me, born the same day and all. I think you need to read the article."

Stunned and saddened as she finished, Katie looked up at Leon.

"This explains a lot," she said. "At the debate, I saw Taylor and you raise your hands when I asked who had a loved one lost due to gun violence. This is so incredibly sad. . . . I have no right to ask you, Leon, but did something happen in your family, too?"

With an expression of despair, he could only say, "I can't, Katie. It hurts too much."

He refolded the article carefully.

Heading back home, all he could think of was the AR-15.

—⁓—

Most nights, Leon and John ate dinner together. John had reduced his stops at fast-food places on his way home so he could support his son's effort to stay healthy. As he drove home from work one crisp autumn day, John thought about selling Grandma's gun range. It was what she'd instructed him to do when she died, in the trust, but he hadn't gotten around to it—too many memories. True, he and Leon used it once in a while, and he knew Leon used it more often, though John had told him not to.

There was something about that AR and Leon. He couldn't figure it out. His son only wanted to use it when he was in a dark place.

Maybe if he sold the gun range and the guns, he could put the money into a retirement plan at the bank and give them a safety net. They wouldn't have to scrape by every month. They could finally make that trip to Disneyland Grandma had encouraged them to take.

At home, John made sure the refrigerator had healthy food in it for Leon. But most days, his truck would pass a 7-Eleven on the way home . . . and so, as was his habit, he pulled into the parking lot, taking his accustomed parking place under an old oak. The old man at the counter smiled, acknowledging him as he went to the same aisle he always did for the package of Oreos he couldn't pass up. He sat in his truck and tore open yet another bag of the creamy/crunchy menaces, knowing they were the reason his belt needed so many notches.

While he munched in the parking lot, he opened the latest edition of his favorite monthly publication, *Guns & Ammo*. Thumbing through the magazine, a picture of a beautiful woman caught his eye.

She looked familiar. Who was she?

He read the text that accompanied her photo. Of course!

She'd berated him that very day, as he'd tried to fix a pipe in her bungalow at the resort. He'd actually *met* this woman that very day.

The article said she was marrying the president of the most powerful gun organization in the country, the same one he'd been a member of for years. He'd carried the worn card in his wallet for decades.

Yes, this was the same woman with the foreign accent. Inna Popov. And the lavish wedding in May would be in Napa Valley, at an unnamed but exclusive resort, so the article said. It went on to say the guest list was sure to include all the notable figures in their organization.

Finishing his last cookie, he took the empty bag to the trashcan in front of the store and dusted the crumbs off his shirt and pants to hide the evidence of his crime and save his belt another notch.

That night at dinner, Leon laughed at John's stories yet again. Whether it was walking a yippy two-pound dog for a diva, cleaning up the "business" of a 150-pound St. Bernard owned by a candy heiress, or adjusting the intensity of a light bulb for a famous violinist, John always had a good story. He loved his job—most of the time.

Leon had stories of his own. Standing at his locker on the north wing of his school, where he'd been shoved and sucker-punched the year before, he told his dad he had stood his ground the day before.

"Right when I was opening my locker to get my lunch out, two older guys bumped into me, Dad. I did just what Coach told me to do—I widened my stance and stared them down. And it worked, Dad. They just walked away!"

Coach had shown him a stance and how to look them in the eyes with an intensity he'd never had the confidence to do before. Along with his added strength, John thought Leon's days of being bullied were over.

When dinner was over, they'd go to the gun range and shoot a few rounds of skeet or target shoot. They used the AR-15 only rarely. Leon secretly thought of it more as a form of stress release, and an effective one.

That night, John, still feeling the unshared sting of his own bully, Ms. Uppity Popov, wondered if he might take solace in the AR. He did, and it helped. Leon took notice.

———

The next morning, John was early to work as usual. He had a lot on his list to do, and he wanted to make sure Ms. Popov was happy. He thought today might be a better day for her, and he was determined to be pleasant and professional, maybe even win her over. After all, she was marrying one of his heroes, a man who had never buckled under pressure. Liberals wanted to take all guns away, and it was his job to make sure that didn't happen. His was an important position.

Clocking in, he recalled dreaming last night that Ms. Popov

apologized to him and gave him a kiss on each cheek. He couldn't help but smile to himself.

Along with the normal work orders that awaited him in his work cubby, a handwritten note from the new general manager asked him to come to his office at 4:00 p.m. That was unusual, but after ten years of employment, he guessed they were going to do something special for him.

Yes, that was it. Being one of The Grape Seed's first employees, and the one with the most tenure, he was excited to find out what the grateful resort managers had in store.

His day was filled with minor repairs to bungalows and a bigger chore: repairing the entrance driveway lighting, which had been damaged thanks to the miscalculation of a guest's Tesla, probably prompted by too much wine-tasting. But, as always, he was able to return everything to tip-top shape. He noticed Ms. Popov, working most of the day with the resort's event coordinator. They'd spent a lot of time at the outdoor wedding site, and he could tell by the exasperated expression on Sammy's face that Ms. Popov was giving everyone a run for their money.

John figured his chance of a heartfelt apology from her was a pipe dream. "Can't win them all over," he said to himself. *At least management knows I'm doing a good job*, he thought.

The day flew by, and John sat in the waiting room outside the new GM's office a few minutes before 4:00. The GM's assistant, Marta Lopez, hustled into the office and closed the door, acknowledging John, but without the "Marta smile" she was known for.

Marta had been at the resort almost as long as John. She'd worked her way up from the bottom, cleaning rooms, doing laundry, and working guest services until she reached her present position. She was easy to admire: efficient, articulate, and well-mannered. John had noted these qualities on many occasions. Nothing had been given to her; she'd earned every step up.

Finally, the door to his office slowly opened. Instead of Marta showing John in, with her head down she walked out past him in silence, a Kleenex in her hand. He was met by the GM at the office door, who then asked him to come in.

John came in and took his seat across the desk from a tall, handsome man, impeccably dressed, someone who could relate to his discerning guests in the one percent.

"John, I'm not going to sugarcoat this for you. A very serious accusation has been made against you by one of our guests."

John all but fell out of his chair. As he shook his head in disbelief, he said, "What happened? What in the world is going on?"

The GM now stood and moved to the side of his desk where he gingerly sat on the edge, looking down at John, as though he'd learned this move in some MBA course. "John, you've been accused of stealing a diamond bracelet from the bathroom of a guest. She has agreed not to get the police involved if we dismiss you immediately. As you know, our resort could ill afford the bad publicity resulting from a situation like this, so I have no choice but to let you go. Marta is preparing your final paycheck and will have it ready as you leave."

John couldn't move, he was so shocked—and crushed. The GM stood and walked to the door to usher John out. There was no "Thank you for your hard work, your ten years of never being late, never missing a day's work," just "Here's the door." Marta couldn't make eye contact with John, and it was clear she'd been crying. She placed the check in his quivering, outstretched hand, cupping it between both of her hands, an attempt to communicate what she couldn't say.

He was almost home when he realized where he was, he was so lost in thought. He just knew it had to have been that bitch, the one from Russia. Marrying his hero.

Maybe that hero shouldn't be on a pedestal after all, choosing to marry a woman like that. This was wife number three, he'd read.

But who was he to judge? He'd married Trina.

He was so distracted by his multiplying thoughts that he drove right past the 7-Eleven. Cookies didn't even matter to him.

He opened a beer and fell into his easy chair, trying to get a handle on what had happened. As he thought about it, his shock became anger.

When Leon arrived home, all ready to tell his dad how Katie had come by PAL today, with cool stories of freshman life at UC Davis, he stopped short. His dad was red-faced, standing next to the entry wall, sheetrock remnants strewn across the hardwood floor. He'd punched a hole in the wall.

Leon put his arm around his unsteady dad and led him to his easy chair. He said, "What the heck happened, Dad?"

As the story came spewing out, complete with the article and pictures of the beautiful bride to be—Inna Popov in *Guns & Ammo*—Leon felt that familiar, creeping feeling rising in his gut.

How could anyone do this to his dad? The retelling of his last two days didn't seem to calm him. No "glass is half-full" conclusions arose. In fact, the events of the day only continued to worsen as John pondered their finances.

He told Leon, "We definitely need to sell Grandma's gun range. We won't get much for it, but anything will help."

Leon helped his dad to bed that night. He'd complained of feeling nauseous, and Leon brought him a wastebasket and wiped his forehead with a cool rag, like Grandma had done for him when he was sick.

"Dad, it will be okay tomorrow. You'll see. We'll figure something out. You are my hero."

But it wasn't okay.

When Leon woke the next morning, he went directly to his dad's room.

He was there, but he was gone. Leon put his hand on the side of his father's neck. It felt cold. He called an ambulance, and everything that followed was a blur.

The autopsy stated myocardial infarction—a massive heart attack.

NINE

In her silky white wedding dress and wavy auburn tresses, she was closing in again, so near this time. Leon was trying to catch up with her, to stop her before she reached his dad, who was sitting in his easy chair, beckoning him to hurry. There was something in her hand, but he couldn't see what it was. He only knew if she arrived first . . .

He awoke with a jolt, bedsheets askew. His heart was pounding as he sat up in bed, alone in the house he'd once shared with the people who loved him. Leon glanced at the clock—it was almost 3:00 a.m. He might as well get up for his 4:30 a.m. shift at Starbucks. Maybe he'd even be on time today. But mostly, he was afraid to fall back asleep and risk the dream again.

Barely eighteen, it had been months since he'd lost his dad—really, he thought, since his dad had been murdered by that Russian bitch. She'd been the one who lied about his dad stealing a bracelet, and without any proof The Grape Seed had fired him from the job he'd loved—fired him with *no proof*. After his dad's funeral, Marta, his work friend, had confirmed the story John told his son that night.

Leon read the *Guns & Ammo* article over and over that his dad had left sitting open on the kitchen table the night before he died. The upcoming May fairytale wedding . . . *How could it be,* Leon wondered, *that this woman could be marrying Scott Pierce, America's point man for gun rights?* The man whose very presence was synonymous with "don't back down or give an inch" had won by an avalanche to lead the most powerful gun lobby in America. Yes, this auburn-haired monster who chased Leon in his dreams was marrying his dad's idol.

Inna Popov was her name.

—⁓—

Inna gazed at the snow-covered park through the floor-to-ceiling windows from her suite at the Four Seasons in Manhattan. The scent of fresh flowers adorning the mahogany coffee table reminded her of her father's garden in spring so long ago. Following close behind as he tended the flowers, holding his hand on meandering walks through their small village—it seemed like a lifetime ago that she did these things. What had happened to the spunky, little brown-haired girl, so naïve and trusting?

What would her father think of her now, she wondered? Even the bathroom in this suite, opulent and modern, was the size of her family's entire living area in Russia. Would he be proud of her successes, her sacrifice . . . or ashamed of her? She wasn't certain. Maybe some of both, she thought, proud at least that she'd survived and thrived in a world where very few did. Inna closed her eyes, blinking back momentary tears, silently berating herself for her weakness.

Her companion, a woman of varied talents, finished sweeping the rooms for bugs. Perfect timing. Inna's handler was knocking on the suite's ten-foot double doors.

Communication between Inna and her handler had been

sporadic and difficult recently, primarily because of Scott's annoying possessiveness of her. It was decided at a much higher level that no phone or email contact would be possible going forward. The degree of sensitivity of their information flow needed to be protected at all costs. Face-to-face was the only solution, and they had much to discuss. Her betrothed was away, speaking at a gun rights convention in Las Vegas, so the covert meeting was set.

The wedding location and date were to remain secret to the public. The wedding, of course, would be small but lavish, held at an ultra-exclusive location—The Grape Seed in Napa Valley. Inna gave the guest list to her anxious handler. As he read the names of Scott's close friends, including a handful of CEOs of major firearms/ammunition manufacturers and a couple of recent southern state additions to Congress—who were only there thanks to his help and influence—he looked at Inna with approval. "Your list is good. Can you add Eagan from Ohio?"

Inna bit her lip, with a now-vivid recollection. "He is sufficiently compromised already. He knows we have photos of him in a—shall we say—delicate situation. You saw them. A wedding invitation could only complicate matters. Is there anyone else?"

The list was finalized. Other than Scott's adored daughter and son-in-law, a powerhouse of gun advocates would be converging in May, cementing relationships and their message.

―⁓―

Coach Padilla, Taylor, and the whole boxing team were in their Sunday best. It was the day of the funeral for Leon's father. The chapel was packed. John's friends, admirers, co-workers were there. Mendy, whom he hadn't seen since middle school, was seated in the front row next to him. She looked the same as she always had.

Most of the people he knew from PAL were there. Katie was seated right behind him, in the second row, black hair in her signature ponytail, wearing the flowered pink dress she'd worn in her debate triumph. She must have returned from college just for this.

The minister at the podium was speaking, but Leon couldn't hear what he was saying until he called his name to come forward and give the eulogy.

Leon stepped forward, ready to talk about his dad, who had meant everything to him—the dad he now idolized. Standing at the podium, he looked out at the audience. A warm feeling enveloped him as he saw the kindness in their eyes, ready to hear his words and share his pain.

As he looked to the back of the room, though, his heart almost stopped. He couldn't speak or shout. He began hyperventilating. With long, auburn hair, in the white silk dress, stood Inna Popov.

Dripping with sweat, unable to move even to kick off his sheets, Leon lay traumatized and alone. Another night plagued by nightmares. Another Starbucks shift out of the question. He supposed he'd probably be fired. He no longer cared.

———

"So, Lewis, if you are accepted into our Rotary Success Scholarship program at Solano College, share with us how you think it will impact your future."

Lewis was thoughtful in his response to this prompt from Roger, one of five Rotarians conducting the numerous interviews. He looked up on the wall behind the Rotarians at a poster that said "Winning doesn't mean never failing; it means never quitting."

Lewis took a deep breath, understanding how much was riding on this fifteen minutes of his life, an interview that could lead to a whole new trajectory for him. He said, "I haven't always made the best choices in my life. Some cost me dearly. Have I had an easy life? Probably most would say no. But I *know* this opportunity with Rotary can change my life. I can be someone who helps others, who can be depended upon. I want more than anything to be a teacher." Glancing up at the poster again, he added, "If you give me this chance, I won't quit. I will make each of you proud."

As the relieved Lewis exited the interview room, another nervous young man was seated outside, awaiting his interview. Lewis patted his friend Taylor on the shoulder and gave him a worn look of encouragement. Nine students, mostly good friends, were vying for three spots—three would receive the magical key to door number three, complete with tuition, books, computer, tutoring, food, and a Rotary mentor.

Taylor had his heart set on being a fireman—someone who helped people in crisis, like he'd been helped. He'd been active in the Fire Explorer program through high school and was one of the youngest ever to be certified in CPR. His dad, Tom, always encouraged him to follow his heart. He'd said that if he was determined to be a fireman, he'd be an exceptional one. With a degree from Solano College's Fire Academy, Taylor was certain he'd have that opportunity. He had talked with Tom about the costs of schooling, and although they could probably make it work, the scholarship would be an incredible gift, one he really hoped to win.

After Taylor's interview, as the Rotarians had done each time, they discussed his competencies. Dr. Richard Lubman had a concerned expression as he looked around at his fellow Rotarians. "We've completed seven of our nine interviews. This is going to be impossible

. . . how can we possibly say 'no' to any of these worthy students? Not one is looking for a handout, only a hand up—an opportunity for a life that will be unavailable to them without this scholarship. Damn it. I, for one, didn't know what I was signing up for when I volunteered to be on the interview panel. How are we going to do this?"

The Rotary Club had resources and funds for three life transformations. No matter how difficult, the decisions would have to be made. But not tonight, the drained panel decided. They'd talk again the next week.

Originally, back in February, ten seniors had signed up to interview for the scholarships. Leon, with the prodding of Ms. Heather, friends, and their fellow "triplet," Taylor, had filled out an application. Katie, though consumed with college in Davis, had even dropped by PAL for the sole intent of making certain both Taylor and Leon had completed their applications for the Rotary scholarships.

When Leon's father passed away so unexpectedly, he'd stopped coming to PAL. It was a week after the tragic death that anyone at PAL even found out about it. Leon didn't contact a single person. Except for Leon and the man from Rockville Cemetery, the small graveside service was attended only by two of John's co-workers. Leon's hurt was so profound and overwhelming, he could barely get out of bed to attend the graveside service himself.

Grandma had made the cost of burial easy. She'd purchased the whole thing in advance, he'd discovered. He was grateful for that. Leon thought that at least she had company now. He looked down as they lowered the casket into the ground.

And then it hit him. Now he was totally alone.

Leon's phone went directly to voicemail when Taylor tried to call him. No return call was forthcoming. Then all his friends heard was "voicemail is full." Many from PAL were worried about him. What would he do now? Did he have the ability, at barely eighteen, to support himself? Was there anything they could do to help?

A few people even knocked on his door. No answers, no response.

With a small life insurance policy and Grandma's unused Disneyland money, he figured he could make it a few more months. Leon dropped out of school three months before graduation and started working at Starbucks—the early shift. He didn't understand much of what was happening around him, only that a bank kept writing, saying they would take away his home.

And it was all her fault. Inna Popov. Everything that was going wrong was because of her.

Wearing his dad's key ring, he went to the gun range. The familiar key fit perfectly. He pushed the dent-riddled metal door to the gun room open, once again.

Anxiety rose in him. He picked up the AR-15. A pistol wouldn't do, this time.

He ripped the wedding page out of *Guns & Ammo*, affixed it to the target, and sent it downrange. He aimed and opened fire. Within seconds, there was nothing left of Inna Popov or the article about her. *She'll have to miss that wedding of hers*, he thought—the one with the secret location.

I know where it will be, he assured himself. He put another clip in the rifle.

A feeling of exhilaration rolled over Katie. Her last final was done before summer break and she'd already accepted a paid summer intern position with Congressman John Garamendi's Woodland office. Before her interviews, Katie had carefully reviewed the duties and expectations of the opportunities before her. Most were similar to one another—opening and sorting mail, responding to constituents, compiling daily news clips. At Mr. Garamendi's office, however, it also included policy research—and that fascinated her.

She packed her bags and loaded them into the ten-year-old Honda Civic her grandmother, Bella, had given her for high school graduation. With the music cranked up, she sang all the way home to Fairfield. There was a lot on her agenda to do before she left in a few days, this time for Sacramento!

Maria peered through the kitchen window at Katie and Bella standing side by side in the backyard. Bella was holding her cane with one hand, Katie's hand with the other. As they walked around the garden, brimming with colorful blooms and intoxicating aromas, both were fully in the moment. The feeling of peacefulness they shared that day would remain a part of Katie and would be something she endeavored to share with many others.

On Katie's agenda was lunch with Betty Lam. Betty had invited her to speak at the Tuesday Rotary meeting and update the club on her progress. The whole club, through Betty's stories, had basically adopted Katie, and they reveled in hearing of her successes, struggles, and aspirations. Katie knew they'd be delighted to learn of her decision to pursue law school. She also planned to drop by PAL to see Ms. Heather and catch up with her many friends there. She still had the tutoring notebook she'd used to keep track of each student's subject and appointment time over the two years she helped out at PAL—more than one hundred students, many of whom had become her friends.

PAL was busy as Katie entered through the double doors. Students were filling the fresh fruit table, set up next to the entrance. The sound of basketballs pounding the hardwood reverberated down the long hall that led to the boxing arena and computer lab. At the front desk, checking students in, was everyone's favorite person—Ms. Heather. A delighted smile met Katie's as they hugged a warm greeting. "So, how are you?" they asked each other at once.

These two had many things in common, they'd found. Among them was a deep-seated kindness toward young people, coupled with a determination to get things done. Another was the ability to talk and listen at the same time, which they did regularly. Confusing to some, amusing to others, they were both comfortable with their unique form of effective communication, at least between the two of them.

So, in the time it takes most individuals to get through small talk, Ms. Heather knew about Katie's 3.9 GPA, knew she would be interning for Congressman Garamendi that summer, and knew she was worried about her friend and fellow "triplet," Leon. Katie, at the same time, learned that PAL was now averaging an incredible 120 students a day and was feeding the hungry ones a couple of times per week, thanks to the Rotary and Kiwanis clubs. Ms. Heather was also worried about Leon, having actually knocked on his door at home, but to no avail.

Just then a large group of students pushed through the entrance, waiting to check in. Katie knew the drill. She mouthed, "Goodbye, see you soon," and headed down the hallway. Most everyone knew Katie, gave her fist pumps and smiles, and waved. Some asked when she was coming back to tutor. "Someday," she promised. "But for now, I need the tutor myself at college!"

She meant it when she said she'd be back to tutor. She loved seeing the light come on when students began to understand a concept or were able to connect the dots. Hearing about their test scores most of the time filled her bucket. But for now, earning the grades to get into law school was on her priority list—and, of course, learning all she could from the internship.

Katie peeked into the boxing area, hoping to see Taylor. He was in the ring, in full headgear, looking like a pro. "Light on your feet, that's it. Left hook, good. Keep moving, you got it," Coach Padilla hollered. The bell rang, and both fighters returned to their corners, exhausted, sweat pouring off them. "Good job, guys. Both of you are throwing fierce right jabs! We'll continue to work on the footwork next week."

Taylor, though his eyes were stinging from the sweat, recognized Katie and waved. "Can you wait five minutes? Let me take a fast shower so you can stand me," he joked, and she nodded with a thumbs-up.

They met in the computer lab a few minutes later, Taylor showered and smelling of cologne he'd borrowed. Katie still didn't understand why so many young men seemed to add cologne to their wardrobe when she was around. The two friends caught up with everything that was going on, Taylor sharing his close call with the gun in his father's truck and how it all worked out. "I kept thinking, Katie, when it was all over, about the debate you won on gun control. And how if guns weren't so plentiful and easy to get, that wouldn't have happened. It almost ended my dreams, and I had nothing to do with any of it."

"Wow, Taylor. I'm sorry that happened to you. It must have been so frightening. Thank heaven for Tom."

They sat in silence for a while.

"Have you heard about this year's Rotary Scholarship winners yet? I interviewed last week, along with eight others. We're supposed to hear soon which three will win. I really want it, Katie, because I don't want to get into Solano's Fire Academy and have to borrow money from my dad and mom. But then, if I get one of the three spots, that means someone else won't be able to go. You know, most of our friends here have no other resources. They won't be able to go, period. So I'm hoping I get it, but also kind of hoping it goes to someone else."

Katie was quiet for a bit and then said, "Taylor, I'm so impressed with you. What a good guy. No matter what, you will be a firefighter someday, and one with a big heart. I'm glad we are friends . . . triplets, right?" They fist-bumped. Taylor had been hoping for a hug. "Speaking of triplets, have you heard anything from Leon? Ms. Heather said since his dad died, he hasn't been coming to PAL, and no one has been able to talk with him."

"Yeah, his phone is disconnected. Maybe he has a new number? When we heard about his dad, we tried to call but no answer. Coach felt bad too. He said we should have gone to the funeral, but it was already over when we heard what happened. I'm worried about him. Do you want to drive out to his house with me?"

Katie said her goodbyes to her friends and Ms. Heather, who was busy at the front desk. Two of the "triplets" headed to check on the third. As they knocked on Leon's front door, they could see his Ford Taurus parked at the side of his house.

Taylor nudged Katie to look at the car—it was no longer that gleaming car that Leon was so proud of. In fact, it looked like it had been off-roading, with mud caked around the wheel wells. The front yard had weeds waist-high.

They knocked again. Still no answer, but both were determined; they weren't leaving until they spoke with him. There was a faint sound of gunfire. Maybe *Fortnite* was playing inside. "He's in there, should we yell for him? If he knows it's us, he'll come to the door. Right?"

They did, and he did. Leon cracked the door just enough that they could see him.

He was almost unrecognizable. His eyes and cheeks had hollowed, giving him a corpselike appearance. His arms were devoid of fat, but he still had the muscles of an eighteen-year-old. Katie and Taylor stood dumbstruck on the porch, neither knowing what to say.

At last, Leon smiled. "It's good to see you." After a long silence, he added, "I've missed PAL, haven't been back since my dad died. Just wasn't ready to see anyone . . . but I knew you'd come."

Taylor said, "We're so sorry you lost your dad, Leon. We didn't know until after his funeral. We would have been there."

"Are you okay? We're all worried about you," Katie added. The three were quiet for a while, not quite sure what to say.

"Yeah, I'm okay. I'm just taking it one day at a time. It's been four months, two weeks, and six days. . . . I was working at Starbucks, but I got fired. I quit going to school too—I was sick of it. My big problem, I guess, is that I can't seem to sleep—and I've run out of money. But it will get better."

Katie was standing so she could see just beyond Leon into the house. He saw she was staring inside and moved to block her view. He could tell she'd seen the arsenal of firearms covering the otherwise empty table.

He stepped out onto the porch and closed the door behind him. "I'm selling my guns to get money to pay the bank so they don't take my house. That's why they're on the table. Money is really tight, but I'll make it."

"Leon, you need help. We're your friends. What can we do?" Taylor almost begged.

"It's all going to work out. I have a plan. . . . It's good to see you again." He suddenly seemed more guarded, but they could tell he was still touched that they had come to see him. "Please tell Coach I said thanks for everything."

And then Leon turned around, went inside, and closed the door. No hugs or goodbyes.

Taylor and Katie walked silently back to the car, with an eerie feeling in the pits of their stomachs. Had they looked back again, they might have seen Leon peeking through the shades, tears streaming down his emaciated face.

As they drove away, the two knew they had to do something.

—⁓—

The control tower at the small and exclusive airport in Napa Valley had been busier than usual this Friday. Eighteen arrivals were scheduled over a two-hour period in the early afternoon, forcing Nate, the ground crew of one, to call in help. NetJets, with their fleet of sleek and luxurious flying taxis used by the rich and famous, was just landing a Citation Longitude.

In fact, as the head of the ground crew had specified to his guys today, NetJets had nine landings. "Wedding season has begun," he'd said. The seasoned group knew this meant good tips, a few star sightings, a crazy story or two to add to their list, and almost guaranteed, at least one real SOB.

The black limo pulled up close to the ramp as the four relaxed and jovial passengers began deplaning. Nate helped the flight crew load the Louis Vuitton luggage into the trunk, along with a leather garment bag. Scott Devlin, with his chiseled good looks and graying dark hair, stepped off first. He held his hand up to steady a smiling young woman,

Alissa, carrying her sleeping three-year-old cherub as she tiptoed down the steps. Whispering, she said, "Daddy, this is so fun! Thank you for bringing Dan and me on the jet. We'll never forget this trip. And hopefully, this one will be your last wedding! You know, it will be hard to go back to the regular airlines after this." The pretty young woman was followed by her husband, Dan, carrying his oversized backpack and his wife's pink Coach purse.

Mr. Lassiter, actually Ross P. Lassiter III, lingered at the top of the steps and signed some documents for the pilot as they chatted. Nate recognized him from a prior visit to Napa Valley. He smiled and knew this was his lucky day—he was the best tipper he'd ever helped. Tanned, tall, and supremely confident with a hawkish intensity, this third-generation owner and CEO of the second-largest firearms manufacturer in the U.S. was used to traveling with NetJets.

And he was used to bringing along all manner of beneficial connections. The primary one today was his long-term devotee, now head of the manufacturers' most powerful quasi-PAC, *Guns & Ammo*: Scott Devlin. He was groom to the vivacious and beautiful Inna Popov.

Ross, who was known, among other things, as a shrewd negotiator with a talent for controlling the bottom line of his flourishing international company, sold the corporate jets a few years prior and instead utilized the more modern and agile NetJets for his travels at half the cost. What he was better known for, however, according to a recent article in the *Washington Sentinel*, was the power he wielded behind the scenes on gun control legislation. Old-school Congress knew that if you crossed Lassiter, then good luck getting reelected.

The article went on to say, "The consequence of his power and that of others with similar sentiment, meant seemingly tough new laws would be passed, keeping the electorate appeased . . . but with the loopholes of a sieve." What the writer from the *Sentinel* suspected but hadn't been able to corroborate was the simple reasoning that the more guns sold, the more money and power for manufacturers, and to hell with the human consequences.

Nate met Ross on the way down from the jet, eager to be of help. "Welcome back to Napa Valley, Mr. Lassiter. We've moved the luggage to your limo already, and I've informed your driver that he'll be taking you up-valley to The Grape Seed. Any special instructions for me, sir?"

"Yes, Nate. Three more jets will be arriving shortly with our group. Please make sure they receive the same good service you've given me."

And he pressed multiple bills into Nate's waiting hand. The top one was a hundred, and Nate hoped the rest were, too.

"Thank you, sir. You can count on it. We have several arrivals today. Where are the flights originating?"

"Two from D.C. Six or seven passengers per jet, I think a few are children. One will originate in Mobile, Alabama. All are VIPs, Nate. Don't let me down."

"No, sir. I'm on it. See you on the turnaround." He closed the door of the limo.

—⁓—

Inna and her assistant had arrived at the resort a few days earlier to make sure all of the details were perfect. Surprised by her jitters, she thought marrying Scott Devlin would probably be the closest she'd get to a normal life.

Yes, she had a job to do, but he was a side benefit, handsome and smitten with her charms. She would have preferred Ross Lassiter, but Scott would do. Tomorrow was her wedding day, and she would enjoy it.

The wedding coordinator from the resort walked the property with Inna again. "You are so fortunate. The weather tomorrow is supposed to be magnificent: eighty-two degrees at noon when you'll be walking down the aisle. The music trio will be located right here, next to the wedding gazebo. They'll begin playing Stravinsky, as you selected, at eleven, while your guests mingle. The thirty-two chairs, flowers, and final touches will be added early tomorrow morning. All will be ready for your most beautiful day!"

She was poised, ready to receive the expected flak from Inna, which she'd suffered many times before. But today there was none. Maybe this wedding would come off as planned after all. Then she could close the book on her "Inna issues."

As they walked across the truly lovely grassy area surrounding the ornate gazebo, Inna realized she was wearing the diamond bracelet, the same one she'd accused that obnoxious chubby man of stealing months before.

Was it a tinge of guilt she was feeling? When she discovered it in the side pocket of her makeup case back in New York, she contemplated calling the resort manager to let him know, but nixed the idea. The man, whatever his name was, had probably been fired already. And, anyway, he was inconsequential—just like most Americans she'd met. The handful that mattered, such as Ross Lassiter, led the others around by an invisible nose ring, including her betrothed. She couldn't resist a giggle at the thought. Soon Inna would be leading Ross around by his nose ring.

Inna brought herself back to the moment at hand, as she had been trained to do. *Tomorrow will be a memorable day*, she thought. Yes, Inna Popov, sweet little girl from the village of Troitsk, Russia, was actually getting married in Napa Valley.

After Katie and Taylor left, Leon wiped his face and eyes and sank into his dad's easy chair. From the adjacent end table, he picked up for the hundredth time the tattered May issue of *Guns & Ammo*. There she was again, standing behind Scott, with her long auburn hair. She was the one who dominated his relentless nightmares.

There on the table was also his to-do list, done on paper rather than with his cell. Leon had written it meticulously over the last month, trying his mightiest to think of every detail. He figured Grandma would be proud of him, at least for making a good list.

With his grandma's last hundred-dollar bill, he put twenty dollars of gas in his car and drove through the car wash.

Check.

The grocery store carried Dad's Root Beer in glass bottles—his dad's favorite too, as it happened.

Check.

Walmart had a sale on ammunition, 100 rounds for fifty dollars—what a deal. That added to his existing stock and gave him plenty.

Check.

He even had enough money left for his favorite deli sandwich.

It was closing in on sunset when Leon arrived home. As he drove into the driveway, he saw something attached to his front door. He grabbed the carefully wrapped remainder of his salami and swiss sandwich and trotted up his porch steps. The pink paper affixed to his door flapped wildly in the wind. Aware it couldn't be good news, supported by the last several months, Leon decided not to let it ruin his mood. "I'm not even going to read it," he told himself, as he let the wind take charge. Mesmerized, he watched the paper fly into the thorn bush, flit over the weeds, and then lift up as though headed for the heavens, only to be violently swept back down to earth and slammed against a block retaining wall. *Thud.*

He winced as though the pain were his own.

No *Fortnite* or TV tonight, period. Comcast had officially cut off his service, the third reminder of his two-month bill crumpled in the trash. Somehow it didn't matter tonight to Leon. That acid feeling in the pit of his stomach wasn't there.

As he closed his eyes, comfortable in his dad's reclined easy chair, he slept all night, no heinous nightmares, no one chasing him.

Meanwhile, the tattered pink paper he'd watched in the wind so intently lay motionless. It was caught in a crevice of concrete and muck, likely its final resting place. Barely still legible was the report number 2018-6204 under the words *Fairfield Police Department—wellness check.*

Officer Oviatt had been dispatched earlier in the day. Two highly concerned young people had reported apprehension regarding the safety of their friend, Leon Phillips—eighteen years old with an arsenal of firearms on his dining room table. The officer felt in his bones that an intervention was critical, but frustratingly, the law didn't allow it. With no record or warrant, no crime committed, all he could do was leave a pink report on the door.

The staff at The Grape Seed that beautiful Saturday morning were busy putting on the finishing touches for the wedding. Additional chairs had been ordered at the last minute, now totaling forty. Another VIP from Washington, D.C., along with her family, was en route, expected to arrive anytime. Rumors were circulating that three U.S. congressmen and one senator would be in attendance, but their names were kept off the record.

Inna looked in the mirror, hair and makeup completed. She'd fretted over how to wear her hair, settling on a chic chignon style, with her hair softly pulled back off her shoulders. *Striking*, she thought as she stared at a face she barely recognized.

Yes, she was pleased. This would do.

In her bungalow, her personal assistant was zipping up Inna's ivory lace and tulle Gucci dress with its plunging neckline. She was almost ready to walk down the aisle.

Stravinsky's *Firebird* had begun, played expertly by the trio on the grass. The formidable Washington guests were only too anxious to mingle with industry leaders represented by the man of the hour—Scott Devlin. Millions of dollars in PAC money and support had come their way, and each of them was determined to keep that spigot flowing. As powerful hands were shaken, and dresses admired, children played merrily in the large expanse of lush grass surrounding the gazebo and chairs.

Right on schedule for the twelve o'clock start, the wedding planner collected the participants. Three-year-old Cecilia, yellow bows in her blonde hair, would walk down the aisle first, accompanied by a Congressman's five-year-old grandson, who was missing his first tooth. Scott's only child, Alissa, would walk next, having agreed to be the only bridesmaid. And, lastly, Ross Lassiter would escort Inna Popov down the aisle, the irony missed by all except her.

Guests all seated, the music changed to traditional. Everyone turned to watch the two precious children, with their angelic smiles, step from the grass to the carpeted aisle. The two ambled to the front, to the sound of admiring remarks from everyone seated. Alissa, in a flowing peach silk gown and with the smile she'd had to practice, hands clasping a matching bouquet, graced the aisle next.

The wedding march was about to begin. The guests were on their feet.

———

Leon had arrived at 10:00 a.m. on that warm and sunny Saturday. It was his third time back in the last few weeks, and he was glad the rainy season was over. He hated getting mud on his car.

The heavily wooded picnic location was fifty feet from the single-lane road that wound up the mountain behind the resort. He parked the Taurus just off the road, hidden from unexpected travelers.

Although the oak trees and shrubs had grown a bit since last summer when his dad had surprised him with another celebrity sighting event, it was still perfect for viewing the gazebo area a few hundred yards below. And he knew for sure this was the place—a Dad's Root Beer bottle, the sign of happier times, had been accidentally left behind as proof.

Leon unloaded the car. He still marveled at the size of the Taurus trunk. Three full loads of stuff fit easily.

At the top of the heap was the quilt Grandma had made, his favorite blanket. He grabbed it, the binoculars, and his dad's nearly threadbare lawn chair and pistol, making sure to close the trunk softly. The clearing he'd claimed was the perfect place to set up both his blanket and the chair. Although thick foliage covered the hillside, this spot was well hidden and still allowed for an unobstructed view of the busy gazebo area below. They would never see him.

His second trip to the car was for a Styrofoam ice chest filled with Dad's Root Beer, the last remaining apple, and part of his deli sandwich, left over from last night, along with the Walmart bag. It was heavy, filled to the brim with ammunition magazines.

Leon opened the trunk for the third time, glancing around to make certain he was alone. There were only a few more items to carry to the clearing: a rickety tripod (the best one he owned) and two assault rifles.

Guns resting on Grandma's quilt, Leon opened the ice chest he'd placed next to his chair. Beads of sweat dripped down his face.

His throat was dry. He downed the icy bottle of root beer, glad he'd bought a six-pack. The half-sandwich sat unopened. *Maybe later*, he thought. He closed his eyes and drank in the quiet around him.

Gingerly clutching his grandpa's gold cross, his chin dropped slightly.

There was Grandma. She was holding him by his shoulders, looking straight into his wide eyes, saying . . . something, but he couldn't hear it. And his dad was there, sitting in his easy chair, despondent—a picture of the auburn-haired devil in his hand.

He woke with a start. Music was playing far below.

Leon rubbed his bewildered eyes. He figured he was only asleep for a few minutes. *What was it Grandma was trying to tell me?*

He shook his head, clearing the cobwebs. *It doesn't matter now, anyway.*

It was time to concentrate. With the binoculars, Leon scanned the grassy area below. Where was she?

He recognized Marta, his dad's co-worker, as she was busily attending to last-minute details. He hoped she wouldn't be there long. The peculiar music played on as children amused themselves and consequential people mingled.

The tripod rested on the quilt. *If I'd had extra money*, Leon thought, *I would have purchased a new one.*

He'd have to make do. Two of the legs were wobbly. A couple of rocks should help that.

Binoculars poised again, he observed waiters in fancy suits carrying silver trays, just like the celebrity weddings he'd watched as he'd sat next to his dad in the very same clearing. Leon wondered if rich people's food tasted better than what everyone else ate. He didn't know, as he'd eaten some really good food "back in the day." He watched as a lady he recognized from the resort interrupted several of the guests, including a couple of small children, to usher them to an adjacent cottage. This meant it was time for Leon to get ready.

The Windham AR-15 was his first choice, spring-loaded with the two-stage trigger he liked best—control to the last nanosecond. He figured he wouldn't need the Smith & Wesson, but he had it just in case.

Leon readied the first magazine with the other three lying next to him. Thirty shots would go fast, maybe in a minute. He would need to reload quickly.

Lying on his belly now, he was ready. The gun was resting on the tripod. He waited.

In his mind's eye, there was Grandma again, trying desperately to tell him something. *Why is she bugging me now?* He thought, *These people deserved what they were going to get. Well, most of them anyway.* The bile burned his throat, and he lay poised to pull his trigger past the point of no return.

He tried to focus. Grandma was still trying to tell him something *. . . what the hell?*

Down below, the music stopped. Leon watched as everyone stood, turning their attention to the back.

There she was . . . every auburn hair in place.

The "Wedding March" began.

Leon's heart was pounding as he adjusted his elbows on the uneven surface, the gun firmly in his grasp. Trembling finger on the trigger, left eye closed, now in the zone, he watched as Inna stood motionless holding the arm of a tall, dignified-looking man. They stood confidently, smiling, at the edge of the red-carpeted aisle.

And then it happened.

A salty bead of sweat dripped into Leon's open eye. He couldn't ignore the stinging . . . or the distinct vision of his grandma saying, "They aren't worth it, Leon. They aren't worth it. Don't do this."

Stunned, his mind was swirling with disjointed thoughts. His sister, Sara, was on a beach, waving at him. Coach Padilla was encouraging him as he punched the bag with his left. Taylor and Katie were eating dinner with him at PAL . . . why was he even here today? Grandma was right.

In the end, the decision wasn't his to make.

The stark reality was that a troubled eighteen-year-old had a loaded AR-15. It was as simple and deadly as a spontaneous jerk caused by another bead of sweat. His right forefinger inadvertently squeezed just hard enough to send the first round flying. Then he couldn't stop . . .

EPILOGUE

Katie Gonzalez closed the massive oak door leading to her D.C. office. Even now, after all the years working in this town that wielded such immense power, she still felt humbled and grateful to play her part. And she still carried the clear stone given to her by Ms. Heather at eighteen years old, as a "gratefulness reminder." *Quiet at last,* she thought. It had been a long day on the Hill, and she had a big day ahead.

Katie coveted her reflection time, that time after her staff had gone home when the phones were quiet. Sitting on the leather couch in her office, her shoes kicked off, she sat mesmerized once more at the significance of her view: the Washington Monument and the Lincoln Memorial. Whenever she felt as though she might be losing her way, or her focus on what was really important to her California constituents and to America, her view brought her back to center. Tonight she needed it.

On the heavy mahogany end table next to her couch sat several sentimental photos. Katie picked up the one with she had framed herself, being careful not to overshadow the photo with the wrong frame. It was of a garden, magnificent in its colors. Standing to the side, leaning ever so slightly on her cane, was Bella, her grandmother.

The loss of Bella had not been easy. Katie smiled at the thought of her own garden in her Suisun Valley yard back home. She smiled every time she thought of her peppers, though now being tended by others.

She carefully replaced the photo and picked up another. This one was of a handsome young man, in full dress uniform of the Fairfield Fire Department, receiving the Rotary Firefighter of the Year Award. Sandwiched between two proud fathers, Tom and Michael, was her lifelong friend. He was now the fire chief, and her frequent advisor over the last many years. How many times had she called on him for his counsel on really tough matters? She couldn't guess. She would be picking him up at the airport tomorrow.

Feeling nostalgic, Katie grasped another photo from the end table. She was wearing the elegant, form-fitting wedding dress that she wished still fit her. Looking into her eyes was the man she adored most in the world, Gabe Diel, her husband and best friend. She checked her phone and confirmed he'd be arriving in a few hours into Dulles International. As a sports commentator on NBC and Google, soccer season was his busy time of the year. Though they were very independent people, when she communicated that she needed him, he moved heaven and earth to be there for her. And this was one of those rare times.

Katie looked up at the wall by her window. Next to her framed Georgetown Law Degree hung her most cherished gift, encased behind glass, with a silver frame she'd painstakingly selected. With embossed lettering she could still read across the room, it said "The Real Power of America Is in American Voices." Three American flags, precisely folded into triangles, surrounded the saying. They were from the flag-draped coffins of three precious children, one black, one Hispanic, one white. All three were murdered in senseless gun violence by another vulnerable young man who'd been incited by hateful rhetoric. The piece was signed at the bottom:

To the Future Senator Gonzalez,
Lest you forget the importance of what you do.
Taylor, 2022

It turned out that Taylor was prophetic on two counts. Katie had made it her life's passion to work for sensible gun laws—and yes, she was Senator Katie Gonzalez from the great state of California.

She thought about the senseless deaths of twenty-six people in Napa Valley, twenty-seven if you counted Leon's suicide, some thirty years ago.

Though only the tip of the iceberg, trumped by so many atrocities in schools, churches, and public venues, The Grape Seed massacre was credited as the turning point for gun legislation. The loss of two sitting Congressmen, three CEOs of gun manufacturers, and even the head of the formidable gun lobby, along with their family members, had a profound effect on the dynamics in D.C.

It had become personal for all of America.

With close to fifty thousand Americans dying every year due to senseless gun violence, each with heartbroken families and communities, America had had enough. Voices were heard loud and clear, and not thousands but millions demanded action from their government.

The groundswell grew across America—through communities rural, urban, and suburban; rich, poor, and that vast majority in the middle; conservative and liberal, young and old. The voices of Americans, of voters, were at last united: "We will accept nothing less than major gun control legislation . . . with teeth."

Individual members of the House and Senate understood they could no longer hide behind platitudes of "It's complicated" or "We must wait until the emotions are level"—both of which were euphemisms for "We're going to let this die down and do nothing." They were forced to act, and they did. And, truth be known, most were relieved to do what was right, especially when the tide turned.

———

It was a magnificent spring day in Washington, D.C., befitting the unveiling of the nation's newest monument—dedicated to those lost to gun violence in America. The monument was immense, stretching nearly a mile, curling around as an imperfect circle. Each state was represented, each name of the innocent accounted for, with nearly two million in all. Some were immortalized on the wall, while others on ground bricks surrounding it. It had been a massive project, one that Katie and so many others had fought hard to fund.

Second-term California Senator Katie Gonzalez stood before the huge crowd at a podium set near the entrance. Her speech was being streamed to millions. She glanced over to catch the eye of her husband and of her dear friend, Taylor. Both were mouthing "You can do this, Katie." Each knew how emotional, how seemingly endless and grueling the fight had been.

She began, "I want to thank each of you for being here. This Monument is for YOU and every American, especially those who have suffered personally due to gun violence. We're here today because of your unrelenting support and generosity.

"Most importantly, today we want to celebrate a milestone. For the first time ever, U.S. deaths due to firearms has fallen below that of most developed countries! This didn't happen overnight. It took us thirty long years. Incremental changes—including Red Flag, Federal Background checks without loopholes, buybacks for all high capacity weaponry—were among the most significant changes and have brought us to today. We progressed from fifty thousand lives lost per year and over five hundred mass shootings in 2019 to twelve hundred with no mass shootings in the five prior years. Still not good enough, but a far cry from where we started." The roar from the crowd was deafening.

Katie continued, "And all of this is because of YOU. You held huge rallies, stormed Congress, and made sure your voices were heard at the ballot box. This Monument bears the names of two-year-olds shot by intoxicated fathers, the five- and six-year-olds murdered at Sandy Hook Elementary, high school students in every state, people worshipping in churches, synagogues, mosques or enjoying a music festival. Wealthy and poor, Republicans and Democrats—every single community has felt the trauma and heartbreak of gun violence. We, together, said NO MORE greed and selfishness at our collective expense. In closing, thank you for allowing me the privilege to work for you— to work for all Americans. May God bless each of you."

ACKNOWLEDGMENTS

At the risk of having deserved acknowledgements exceed the length of my first novel, I'll try to keep them brief.

First, thank you, Service Club members, for your earnest inspiration in helping our communities, simply for the sake of making our world a better place for all. In particular, Rotary's guiding principles of truthfulness, fairness, kindness and helping others serves us as a beacon to strive toward, which is perhaps never more important than now.

Rotary friends, thank you for your encouragement, your inspiration as human beings, and for serving as role models. Without each of you, writing this novel would have been impossible. Dear friend and seasoned author, William Wesley, I appreciate your savvy advice and motivation. Ron Turner, retired police officer and now advisor to Senator Bill Dodd, thank you for your guidance and sage ideas on the ending of the novel. (I listened!)

Kudos to the entire PAL (Police Activities League) organization for serving as an irrefutable example of tangibly helping others—one starfish at a time. The pain of losing one is never forgotten. And the joy of positive outcomes feeds their soul to continue making a difference.

A very special thank you to two young people. I am privileged our paths crossed. In their own ways, now daughter, Cortney, and

PAL member, Lewis, both inspired and contributed to this endeavor, demonstrating perseverance and goodness.

To my parents, Jane and George Wooden—your consistent encouragement to reach for the stars, always being on my side, and believing in me made me into the person I am. I wish for everyone to experience the support I've been so fortunate to have.

Dave, husband and biggest supporter, thank you for the countless interruptions to "run something by you" as this novel evolved. You never once made me feel as though I were bothering you, and you never ceased to encourage me, knowing the topic must have given you pause. I love you forever. For my daughter and son-in-law, Shannon and Brock, your help with technology made this novel complete. Without your help, I would still be looking for the revisions. And my grandchildren, Khloe, Gabe, and Luke—now I can return to being your "Gee Gee," without you having to hear "Can't, because I'm working on my book."

Rob Foreman, editor extraordinaire, thank you for your subtle nudging and astute guidance. You made the journey delightful.

ABOUT THE AUTHOR

Tara J. Dacus is a successful business owner, wife, proud mother and grandmother, and active Rotarian. Through her extensive volunteer work, she has become passionate about the critical importance the community plays in the well-being and success of its youth. After becoming aware of how the lack of consistent sensible gun laws undermines the good being done across our nation, Tara is committed to helping to eliminate gun violence.

CPSIA information can be obtained
at www.ICGtesting.com
Printed in the USA
FSHW011316291219
65193FS